THE FAITHFUL HEART

Tamzin and Laura Thornham's father had converted their country house in Devon into a hotel some years before. After the business falters, he sells it to Canadian entrepreneur Rob Hunter, extracting a promise that his daughters would always have the right to reside there. When Rob appears to be forming a close friendship with her beautiful younger sister, Tamzin hides her own feelings, aware she might be losing the man with whom she's fallen in love . . .

Books by Janet Cookson
in the Linford Romance Library:

QUEST OF THE HEART
MASQUERADE
TO LOVE FOR EVER

JANET COOKSON

THE FAITHFUL HEART

Complete and Unabridged

LINFORD
Leicester

First published in Great Britain in 1999

First Linford Edition
published 2001

British Library CIP Data

Cookson, Janet
   The faithful heart.—Large print ed.—
Linford romance library
   1. Love stories
   2. Large type books
   I. Title
   823.9'14 [F]

   ISBN 0–7089–5946–6

Published by
F. A. Thorpe (Publishing)
Anstey, Leicestershire

Set by Words & Graphics Ltd.
Anstey, Leicestershire
Printed and bound in Great Britain by
T. J. International Ltd., Padstow, Cornwall

This book is printed on acid-free paper

1

Why on earth had she come? Tamzin glared at the gleaming navy blue paintwork of the locked door, the row of intercoms an unwelcome reminder that the inhabitants of Victoria Wharf were well protected from unwanted visitors.

Finding out his private address from a journalist friend had given her hope that she would, at last, be able to confront him face to face. Now, she realised how naïve she had been. One mention of her name and the door would remain firmly shut against her. She wondered whether to leave, then almost immediately rejected the idea. She'd got this far. She'd give it one last shot.

She jabbed at the bell marked Penthouse only to start as a disembodied voice growled back at her, 'Have you forgotten your key again?'

After a pause which seemed over long to her jangled nerves she replied in the affirmative, tension tightening her throat and husking her voice.

The answering, 'Do you have a cold?' sent a wave of hope through her.

Tamzin prefaced her reply with a hoarse cough.

'Afraid so.'

She hoped she hadn't overdone it, hadn't blown a golden opportunity.

'Come on up.'

The door whirred open and Tamzin was drawn up four flights of stairs to another closed door — the last barrier! Tentatively she pushed at the door, relief sweeping through her as it swung back on its hinges and she entered.

It was like stepping out on to the deck of a ship. Parquet flooring stretched before her to meet huge metal framed windows cut into the far wall. The room was empty and Tamzin crossed to the windows, drawn by the view of the River Thames easing its way past warehouses newly converted into luxury homes.

Reluctantly she turned her back on the fascinating view and began to survey the apartment she had entered on false pretences. The large open floor space was broke up by metal uprights rising to meet iron girders spanning the high, vaulted ceiling, whilst a spiral staircase snaked up to a mezzanine floor. The place looked unlived in, with its bare brick walls and sparse furnishings. Tamzin decided. She compared it unfavourably with her own cluttered but beloved home. She could almost feel sorry for the man if she didn't know him to be such a rat.

'Something medicinal, darling . . . '

The door in the opposite wall slammed shut on the sudden silence as the man came to an abrupt halt.

'Who on earth are you?'

Deftly he unloaded a whisky decanter and tumblers on to a low coffee table and moved closer, his large body moving with controlled strength as his eyes appraised her. It took all of Tamzin's self control to hold her ground. For one week she had stalked Rob Hunter, her sole objective to gain a few moments of his time. Now, she could feel her words deserting her, her eyes held by his quizzical glance as he stopped a few feet from her.

No wonder this maverick entrepreneur from Canada had instilled so much fear into the business world with his notorious but successful property deals. Ruthlessness was evident in the strong features, dark brown brows now drawn together as suspicion fleeted across his face.

'It's you!'

Sudden realisation lightened his tone as his glance encompassed her, taking in the slight figure in jeans and leather jacket, corn coloured tresses drawn up into a pony tail.

'You're the dainty creature who's been following me for the last week,' he went on, 'I thought I was being haunted!'

4

'Just trying to get a chance to speak to you, Mr Hunter.'

'You never thought of asking for an appointment?'

'Thought about it,' she snapped, 'tried it, found it would be easier to get into Fort Knox!'

Unexpectedly he threw his head back and gave a great roar of laughter.

'So, you decided to use a little trickery. Well, as I let you in I'd better hear what you have to say. You have two minutes, little lady.'

'Then I won't waste time. I want to know why you're throwing my sister and myself out of our home after all — '

'Woah, there,' Rob Hunter said, holding up one hand. 'Let's have your name before any more accusations fly.'

'Tamzin Thornham.'

At the sound of her name Rob Hunter straightened, his expression tightening.

'Then I'm not surprised you weren't given an appointment. I didn't want

5

any contact between us, Miss Thornham, because I didn't want to be conned by a member of your family a second time.'

Tamzin could hardly believe what she was hearing.

'What on earth are you talking about? My father worked very hard on your account, Mr Hunter, and what's more he trusted you. He sold you Thornham House on the condition that our family would always have a home there, but now he's gone, we find that you intend to evict us. How much is your word worth now, Mr Hunter?'

'A darned sight more than your father's ever was.'

Rob Hunter took a menacing step towards her and she found herself backing away. He stopped suddenly, his eyes fixed on her face.

'You don't know what I'm talking about, do you?'

'I don't understand why you're so hostile to my father.'

'I think you'd better sit down.'

He gestured towards a cream leather couch and when Tamzin opened her mouth to protest, he forestalled her with, 'You've tricked your way into my home, please have the courtesy to listen to me.'

Tamzin sat down and Rob pulled up a chair opposite.

'When I bought Thornham House, the business was making a loss as your father had over extended himself to convert the house into a hotel. I wanted the property, however, and thought the business had potential. I bought it from your father at a price which allowed him to clear off his debts, and I asked him to stay on as manager. I told him he and his family would always have a home there.'

Rob Hunter grinned wryly.

'I think you would agree I've been more than generous to your family.'

Tamzin nodded silently and Rob continued.

'For a while everything went well. With new capital, the financial position of the hotel stabilised and I was well pleased with my new acquisition. Then I began to suspect that someone was undermining my business activities. Sensitive information was being passed to business rivals. I engaged a private investigator and he traced the leaks to your father.'

'No! That's not possible! Dad would never be dishonest. Besides, he spent all of his time in Devon, at the hotel. How could he know anything of your other business interests?'

'All part of my open approach, I'm afraid. I meet regularly with my managers and let them know how the group is performing. Your father was privy to confidential information. He had ample opportunity to betray me.'

'There must be some mistake,' Tamzin said in desperation. 'The investigator must have got it wrong.'

'I don't think so. You see, your father confessed when confronted with the findings. I have a signed statement to that effect. He was told there would be no prosecution if he left quietly. Two weeks later he had his fatal heart attack. Naturally, I was very sorry to hear of his death but under the circumstances I didn't want any members of your family to continue to live in Thornham House, hence the notice to quit.'

As his words registered, the shock must have shown on her face for Rob Hunter leaned forward, his expression solicitous.

'You look very pale, Miss Thornham. Shall I get you a drink?'

'No, I really must go. I can't take this in all at once. Mr Hunter, I — '

The sound of a door opening and slamming shut cut into her words then a high, shrill voice called out.

'Ciao, darling. Sorry I'm so late.'

Tamzin rose as a tall blonde swung into view clutching a bottle of red wine in her right hand.

'The traffic was awful. Oh . . . '

'I was just leaving,' Tamzin said abruptly.

'Miss Thornham and I have concluded our business.'

Rob Hunter turned from Tamzin to his visitor. He barely acknowledged Tamzin's farewell as she slipped out of the apartment. Once outside she hunched her shoulders against the biting wind and decided to walk back to her hotel. She made a decision to drive back to Devon that very night. There was no point in remaining in London any longer. She had come there seeking answers and had uncovered further questions, but whatever the truth really was, one thing was clear from her encounter with Rob Hunter.

His mind was set against them staying at Thornham House. At the end of the month she and her sister would have to leave their beloved family home, and she had no idea how she was going to break the news to Laura.

Laura's reaction was just as Tamzin had expected.

'But there must be something you can do. Go and see Rob Hunter again,

Tamzin,' Laura pleaded, her heart-shaped face streaked with tears.

Tamzin sighed and turned away. She had relayed as much as she dared to of her London trip to Laura but still her sister refused to face the facts.

'He wouldn't listen, love. His mind is quite made up.'

'But he promised Daddy we'd never have to leave. Perhaps we could go to law,' she went on wildly, 'sue him for breach of contract of something.'

'There was no contract, no binding agreement at all. We've no money for lawyers, Laura, and no case! You've always complained about living in such a backwater,' Tamzin pointed out but Laura refused to be comforted.

Tamzin wandered across to the window to look down on the gardens full of the bloated flowers of late summer. It would break her heart to leave Thornham House but she felt unable to give in to her sorrow just as she felt unable to tell Laura what Rob Hunter had said of their father. She had become her sister's protector when their mother had died when she had been in her teens and had never felt able to relinquish the rôle. Now, faced with the death of their father and the imminent loss of their home, it was more important than ever that she stay strong for both their sakes.

Her gloomy thoughts were interrupted by the sound of their outer door opening and the cheery call, 'Anyone at home?'

'William!' Tamzin called out. 'Come on in.'

A tall, dark-haired young man stepped into the sitting-room.

'Hi, nice to see you back, Tamzin. How did you get on in London?'

Before she had a chance to answer, his eyes had strayed towards Laura's tearful features and in answer to his questioning glance Tamzin gave him a brief resumé of her trip.

'So, we only have a few weeks to find somewhere else to live and I haven't even found a job yet,' she ended.

William grimaced.

'That's really tough. You can always stay at our place, you know. Mum and Dad would love to have you both.'

'Thanks.'

It might well come to that. They had little money and since Dad's death and her return from abroad she'd had no luck in finding work.

'Anyway, I'm here to ask you out to dinner tonight, Tamzin, and after what you've just told me it looks as though you could do with cheering up.'

'I'm sorry, William, but I'm on duty in the hotel this evening. Henry Chapman, Dad's deputy, has been running the hotel practically single handed since Dad died. The poor man's rushed off his feet so I've promised to relieve him.'

'You'll still need to eat, sis.'

Laura broke her silence and flashed her sister an encouraging look.

'Perhaps you and William could have dinner in the hotel dining-room.'

Tamzin pondered her words.

'Well, we're not very busy tonight. Why not?'

They settled on a time and when Tamzin had shown him out and returned to the sitting-room she was met with, 'It's about time you and William went out on a proper date.'

'It's not a date,' Tamzin said defensively, 'just a meal with an old friend.'

'That's not how William will see it,' Laura went on mischievously. 'He adores you. He was devastated when you went off to Paris.'

'I adore him in turn,' Tamzin said easily, 'but we have grown up together. We're more like brother and sister.'

Laura seemed ready to argue the point when a ring on their doorbell distracted both of them.

'Who on earth could this be?' Tamzin said, hurrying to the door.

Henry Chapman rarely invaded their privacy and their only other regular visitor, William, had just left. She opened the door to a tall figure.

14

'Mr Hunter! This is rather unexpected.'

'But not unwelcome, I hope. May I
come in?'

'Of course! This way, please.'

She led him down the short passageway and when he stepped into the
sitting-room, their cosy, familiar room
seemed suddenly to shrink in size.

'What a charming apartment.'

His eyes scanned the room and came
to rest on Laura's exquisite face, a
blush now colouring her cheeks whilst
her green eyes had returned to their
customary sparkle.

'You must be Laura.'

He crossed the room as though
drawn to her side by an invisible
magnet. 'Your father told me all about
you. Even he didn't quite to do you
justice.'

He held out a large, tanned hand.

'I'm Rob Hunter.'

Tamzin smiled inwardly. She was
quite used to being ignored by men
whenever her sister was present. Laura

15

had inherited the black hair of their Italian grandmother, and that, together with the pale skin and green eyes which they both shared proved a lethal combination where the opposite sex was concerned. Laura had now taken his hand and was expressing her pleasure at meeting him, which was not quite what she was saying about him a few moments before! Tamzin coughed discreetly. When Rob Hunter's eyes were drawn to hers she asked him pointedly what they could do for him. His lips curved into a smile.

'I just called to let you know that I'm at the hotel for the weekend at Henry Chapman's request, to look over the books.' His glance strayed to Laura once more. 'I wondered if I could tempt you two ladies to dine with me tonight.'

'Tamzin has a date,' Laura said quickly. 'But I'm free.'

'Good. Then I'll see you at eight.'

He swept out and as the door closed Laura said, 'But he's utterly charming. You made him out to be some sort of monster, Tamzin.'

'He is intending to throw us out of our home,' Tamzin pointed out drily, but Laura was barely listening, her mood transformed from gloom to optimism in as short a time as it had taken her tears to dry.

'I'll have to go through my wardrobe and find something scrumptious to wear,' she declared, and whirled away to leave Tamzin staring at the closed door, her brow furrowed.

What was Rob Hunter really doing here? He'd made no mention of a proposed trip when she'd seen him in London and it seemed strange he should visit so soon after their awkward encounter. Perhaps he intended to supervise their departure in person. The thought made her shudder. Leaving her beloved family home would be difficult enough without Rob Hunter's sneering presence

She expressed her fears to William over dinner, and he tried to allay her suspicions.

'Rob Hunter's group does own the hotel, love. It's only natural he should want to see how it has fared since your father died.'

Tamzin wasn't convinced.

'He said it was at Henry Chapman's request but when I asked Henry he said Rob Hunter rang and suggested a visit out of the blue. I can't help feeling I made matters worse when I went to London. I fear I may have antagonised him.'

'He looks far from antagonised tonight,' William went on drily.

Tamzin followed his glance to see Rob Hunter entering with her sister by his side. Laura looked stunning in a slinky dress in cornflower blue. The admiration in her face was clear for all to see as she looked up at her tall companion.

'They look very chummy for new acquaintances,' William remarked as they seated themselves and began to study the menu together.

Tamzin experienced a stab of anxiety.

'They do, don't they? Rob·Hunter's a lot older than her and obviously more experienced. I hope Laura keeps her feet on the ground.'

'She's not a kid any more, Tamzin. She's twenty.'

'She's still young in many ways,' Tamzin went on defensively.

'Now, listen here, love. You must try to stop mothering her. You're only six years older than her and it's time you thought of yourself for a change and left your kid sister to her own devices.'

'I know,' Tamzin admitted, 'but I've looked out for her since Mum died and it's hard to break the habit.'

'You have to, love. It's time to let go.'

Tamzin knew he was right.

Next day, Laura was fulsome in her praise of Rob Hunter as a charming dinner date but when Tamzin tried to glean some information as to his motives in visiting Thornham House, Laura clearly knew nothing. Tamzin had agreed to relieve Henry in the hotel over the weekend and was in a good position to observe Rob Hunter's movements. To her surprise he seemed to behave like any other guest, rarely leaving the hotel and making full use of its leisure facilities.

He played tennis with Laura in the afternoons but, in spite of their growing friendship, she still seemed none the wiser as to the real reason for his visit. Tamzin concluded that, canny business-man as he was, he was most likely adept at making small talk without revealing too much about himself.

In some respects Rob Hunter's discretion was a blessing, she decided. She did not want Laura to know of their father's alleged misdemeanour and on this subject he had clearly remained silent.

By Monday, Tamzin had worked two long shifts and was looking forward to handing over the reins to Henry. Laura was out riding and she had just made herself some coffee and begun to write some business letters when the house phone rang. She picked up the receiver to hear Rob Hunter's distinctive voice on the line.

'Tamzin?'

When she answered in the affirmative he went on.

'I'd like to see you in the manager's office right away.'

'I'm afraid I've only just come off duty. Could it wait a while?'

'No, it cannot wait. It concerns your future, and your sister's. I'll expect you in five minutes.'

The line went dead and Tamzin replaced the receiver with a frown. What was so urgent that she had to be ordered about like a naughty schoolgirl? Whatever the reason for Rob Hunter's summons, apprehension knotted her stomach at the thought of their imminent encounter.

2

'I'll come straight to the point, Tamzin,'
Rob Hunter said. 'I'd like you to
manage the hotel for me.'

This was the last thing Tamzin had
expected! She struggled to find the
right words.

'I'm very flattered by your offer but I
must warn you that I have no formal
qualifications in hotel work.'

'But you do have experience.'

'Yes, I do,' Tamzin admitted. 'I
helped my father with the initial
conversion here, found I enjoyed the
work, then took up a position in a Paris
hotel to further my experience. Since
my return I've been helping Henry out
but he's borne the brunt of the
responsibility since Dad died.'

Rob Hunter leaned back in his chair,
one hand stroking his chin.

'You're doing your best to try to talk

me out of giving you this job, Tamzin. Why? Does the thought of working for me appal you that much?'

'Of course not! I'm just trying to be completely honest with you.'

'Unlike your father, you mean?'

Colour flooded into Tamzin's cheeks. 'No, I do not mean that!'

She rose abruptly but as she turned away, Rob moved swiftly from behind the desk to detain her, his hand coiling around her wrist.

'I'm sorry, that was uncalled for. Please stay.'

His eyes smiled down at her and Tamzin found herself looking away, her heat skipping a beat. No wonder Laura was falling for him. When he turned on the charm he was well nigh irresistible!

As though sensing her weakening resolve he said, 'Let's sit down and have some coffee. Then we can discuss my proposal more informally.'

She allowed herself to be led to one of the winged armchairs drawn up to a low table and watched Rob pour dark liquid from the vacuum jug.

As though he could read her mind he said, 'I know you must have lots of questions, so fire away. Ask anything you like.'

'Well, what would happen to Henry Chapman? I'd hate to displace someone who's worked so hard for the hotel.'

'You won't be. I intend to make Henry your co-manager. He has the training and experience you lack but although I value him as an administrator I want something more for Thornham House.'

Tamzin's brows rose.

'Which is?'

'Flair. I've done my research, Tamzin. I know that you planned the new decor when the house was converted into a hotel. The result is impressive and I think you can bring the same imagination and panache to running the place. Also, you really love this house and that comes across when you're on duty. You welcome guests as though you're inviting them into your own home. That

24

personal touch is rare in hotel work and I value it.'

Tamzin's cheeks were scarlet. She'd had no idea when she had been observing Rob over the weekend that she'd been the object of his scrutiny in return!

'I'm making a hard-headed business decision,' he went on, 'and I must warn you that my standards are exacting. If you accept this post you and Henry will have to come up with a business plan for next year which will expand our trade and increase profits. What do you say, Tamzin? Do you accept the challenge?'

Tamzin looked across at him, blue eyes sparkling.

'Of course I do!'

When she found Laura to give her the news, her sister threw her arms around her and hugged her tight. Tamzin, laughingly, begged to be released as Laura wondered aloud on the change in their fortunes.

'It's not just the job, sis, this also

means we'll be able to stay here.'

'That's right. Our flat goes with the position.'

Tamzin sat on the sofa and tucked her feet up beneath her.

'All I need to do to ensure we stay here is keep on the right side of Rob Hunter.'

'That won't be too difficult, surely.'

Tamzin grimaced.

'I'm not so sure. Henry and I will have to meet some ambitious targets for this hotel.'

'You'll do it,' Laura said loyally.

'I hope so.'

To her relief, Henry seemed quite happy with their new partnership.

'I know very little of hotel administration,' Tamzin reminded him, 'so I shall have to rely on your expertise.'

Henry suggested they set aside an hour each day in which he would tutor her in hotel procedure. Tamzin agreed happily, eager to learn the ropes as quickly as possible.

After two gruelling weeks, however,

she realised she was learning most practical day-to-day experience as she learned to think on her feet and cope with the unexpected which seemed to crop up on an almost daily basis! In spite of the long hours and demands she was subjected to, however, she began to find her new life exhilarating. She had always enjoyed meeting people and found the social side of her job the most rewarding. She and Henry began to settle quite naturally into their rôles. Henry began to spend more time in the office, dealing with paper work, whilst she began to play a more public rôle in hotel life.

One morning she was thinking about Rob Hunter, about how he had seen qualities in her which she had barely been aware of herself, when the office phone rang. As Rob Hunter's voice crackled in her ear she had the uncanny feeling that her thoughts had conjured him up. She was slow to react until an impatient, 'Is that you, Tamzin?' pulled her up.

'Yes,' she said quickly. 'Good morning, Mr Hunter.'

'Rob, please. Anyway, I've just called to congratulate you. I believe you've settled into your new position very well.'

How did he know? Had he set a private detective on to them again? She thanked him, wondering what the real purpose of his call was but his next words enlightened her.

'Also, I wondered if you could give me an update on the business plan for next year, the one we discussed when I appointed you.'

Tamzin had little memory of what they had discussed. She had been so shocked by his job offer she had barely taken in what he was saying!

'Henry and I have been rushed off our feet,' she said, playing for time, 'but as soon as we have a spare moment — '

'In other words,' he put in, 'you haven't even thought about it!'

'I'm afraid not,' Tamzin admitted candidly.

His sigh was overlong.

'As you're new to the job I'll give you some grace but I'm coming down in a fortnight and I expect to see something on paper. The hotel's in good shape for further expansion and I want some bright ideas from you and Henry on how to do just that. Two weeks, Tamzin, that's all you have!'

On that warning note, the line went dead and Tamzin was left glaring at the instrument. Why did he have to be so high-handed? Surely a little courtesy would not come amiss. She sighed and inwardly had to admit that her ill temper was less to do with Rob's manner and more to do with the fact that she dreaded the task ahead. She had just two weeks to come up with novel ideas on how to expand the business. At this precise moment her mind was a complete blank. She hurried off to find Henry.

Over the next few days they attempted a few brain-storming sessions and she quickly realised that it would be down to her. Able administrator as Henry was he seemed unable to see further than increasing their local trade. Tamzin knew that would not do. Rob Hunter ran hotels of international standing. He may have bought a hotel in a Devon backwater but that would only have been on the assumption that he would be able to raise its profile.

They had few Continental guests at the hotel and Tamzin thought this was a market they could develop. She, herself, spoke fluent French and German and had worked in Paris until recently. The more she thought about expanding the European end of the business the more sense it made. She talked through her ideas with William when they were having pre-dinner drinks at the local pub one evening. He had worked in his family's accountancy firm since graduating and she respected his business sense.

'I think you're on the right track, Tamzin,' he said after she'd finished her explanation. 'I think you've probably exhausted the British end at the moment so it makes sense to look across the Channel.'

'I'm glad you approve,' Tamzin said with relief. 'This is new territory for me. I need all the support I can get.'

'Would you like me to help you put this paper together? I do no end of business reports for Dad. I'd be happy to help.'

'That would be wonderful!'

She smiled into his eyes, suddenly grateful she could rely on his friendship. He leaned towards her, his expression eager, and she found herself looking down at her watch.

'Goodness, is that the time? We'd better hurry if we're to get our seat at the restaurant.'

She slipped off her stool, averting her eyes from his and whilst he was paying for their drinks she wandered outside. As she waited, a red, open-topped sports car screeched to a halt and a fair-haired, stocky man climbed out. Blue eyes swept over Tamzin and came to rest on her face.

'Lovely evening.'

His voice had a sharp, London twang to it and when Tamzin made an appropriate reply he shot her a bold glance before bounding up the steps into the pub. He seemed an unlikely visitor to their quiet local, she decided, feeling strangely disconcerted by their fleeting encounter. She shifted restlessly, wondering what on earth William was doing. She looked idly through the bay window on her right into the small parlour, empty at this early hour save for a girl in the far corner.

The man she had just seen entered with a drink, the girl turning round in greeting. It was Laura! What on earth was she doing with this man? He was much older than her, and was quite unlike the sort of admirer who usually flocked to her side. Tamzin was making a mental note to ask her sister about her date when William returned and ushered her to the car.

Over the next few days Tamzin forgot

all about her sister's choice of date. Rob Hunter was due at the end of the week and she and William spent every evening working on the business plan. William's accounting skills were invaluable in calculating cash-flow projections and financial targets and on Friday evening, after another mammoth session, they were able to put the finishing touches to the report and run a final copy off the computer.

As Tamzin prepared for bed that evening she knew that the next day was a crucial one for her and Laura. Her credibility was on the line and if Rob Hunter found her wanting, her days as a hotel manager and their life at Thornham House would be numbered. An hour later she sat up in bed, too keyed up to sleep. She slipped on her robe and went into the sitting-room where she began to pace about. She felt a need for activity but wondered what she could do which would not disturb Laura at this late hour.

Suddenly she was reminded of her

father's papers. William had sorted out his affairs as best he could but she still needed to go through his accounts. She had put off the task, but as she sat at the desk and began, she found it less painful than she had feared. Thanks to William's preparatory work it was also less complicated and within quite a short space of time she was filing the last bank statement.

As she pushed the folders to one side it struck her, as though out of the blue, that she had found nothing untoward. Surely, if her father had been selling secrets as Rob had alleged, she would have found damning evidence such as deposits of large, unexplained sums of money. Her father appeared to have died, as he had lived, in modest circumstances.

She frowned, fingers drumming on the table top. She had had little time to consider Rob's accusations since he had uttered them and had been too shocked at the time and too ignorant of all the circumstances to mount a proper defence of her father. But now? Why shouldn't she delve further into the mystery Rob had handed her? She couldn't bring her father back but she could restore his good name. Rob Hunter had made a mistake in accusing her father of treachery and she would prove it to him!

Next morning, Tamzin woke late, bleary-eyed. After one glance at her alarm clock she shot out of bed, pulling on her robe as she hurried into the sitting-room to find William pouring coffee into two mugs.

'William! What on earth are you doing here so early?'

'Well, it isn't that early is it, love?' he said matter of factly. 'I thought you might need some moral support. Laura let me in before she dashed off for her early-morning swim or whatever athletic thing she does at this time of the morning. Anyway,' he added, 'have some coffee, I've just made fresh.'

'Bless you,' Tamzin said as she reached for her drink. 'I've had a dreadful night and I feel as though my brain has turned into cotton wool.'

The doorbell rang and Tamzin said in explanation, 'That'll be Henry. We decided on a final get-together before Rob Hunter descends. Let him in, there's a love.'

William complied and Tamzin drank deeply from her mug, eyelids lowering as she breathed in the rich aroma of the brew.

'Good morning, Tamzin.'

Tamzin's eyes flew upwards to find Rob Hunter standing before her, a hapless William beside him, his face a picture. She sat up straight, one nervous hand pulling her robe around her.

'Good morning. I see you've already met William.'

'We haven't been formally introduced. I gather this is a friend of yours.'

He glanced at William, then back to Tamzin, his eyes speaking volumes.

'We were just having coffee,' Tamzin rushed on. 'Perhaps you'd like some.'

'No, thank you, I've no time for social niceties. I've come for the report and I gather from Henry that you have the final copy.'

'It's here.'

Tamzin crossed to the desk then handed over the document. Rob Hunter turned from her, his final words thrown over his shoulder as he swept out of the room.

'I'll see you in the office in one hour, Tamzin.'

They heard the outer door slam shut and then Tamzin looked across at William. His brows rose heavenward and to Tamzin that wordless gesture seemed to say it all.

Exactly one hour later, knocking nervously on the office door, Tamzin could only regret their unsettling encounter earlier that morning. Evidently, he felt the same, for, as she seated herself opposite the desk, he said, 'I'd like to get one thing straight before we get on to business. I expect my senior staff to behave with discretion in their personal lives, especially when they live on the premises.'

'I'm not sure what you mean,' Tamzin stammered.

'To put it in simple English, I don't relish finding young men in your apartment at breakfast-time with you still in your night attire.'

Hot colour rose in Tamzin's cheeks.

'I think you misunderstood the situation. William is an old family friend.'

'Is that what they call it nowadays?' he put in cynically.

'Mr Hunter, I resent your assumption that I was . . . that there was anything . . . '

Her voice trailed away and Rob Hunter took the opportunity to cut in.

'I don't require an explanation, Tamzin. Just remember to conduct your love affairs away from the hotel in future and we'll say no more.'

Shocked by his insolence, Tamzin opened her mouth to protest and then closed it again. What was the point? He was obviously determined to see everything in the worst possible light but the man's hypocrisy really was astounding. How many 'darlings' did he currently have in his life?

Ignoring the silence, Rob turned to the document before him.

'To return to the matter in hand, I've read your report and I'm pleased to say I'm very impressed with it.'

Relief swept over her. Thank goodness she had done something right!

'I'm glad you like it,' she said.

'I'm particularly interested in your suggestion of developing the European market. You're quite correct when you say European guests are under-represented at our hotel. Now, tell me, how do you intend to market Thornham House on the continent?'

'By using my contacts in Paris to obtain the services of a good advertising agency.'

Gaining in confidence as she spoke, Tamzin sketched out her ideas for a marketing campaign to cover northern Europe. As she finished speaking, he nodded his head in approval.

'You seem to have thought this through thoroughly, so go ahead and commission an agency to come up with some proposals. We'll make a final decision on a suitable campaign when we see what they've come up with. Business concluded then I think.'

Tamzin rose hastily as he stood up but as she turned to go Rob said, 'Don't hurry off, Tamzin. I hoped you'd join me in pre-lunch drinks.'

He gestured towards the fireplace where a log fire burned and two chairs had been drawn up before a coffee table set with a sherry decanter and glasses. She supposed it would be churlish to refuse but, seated before the warmth of the fire, glass in hand, she wondered for one panic-stricken moment how on earth she was going to make small talk with Rob Hunter.

'Don't look so apprehensive,' he said, with that uncanny knack he had of echoing her thoughts. 'I asked you to have a drink to help break the ice between us, that's all.'

If there was ice between them it was of his making, she decided silently. He had begun their meeting by accusing her of running some sort of bawdy house and ended it by praising her professional skills! Still, he was her boss and had granted her a wonderful opportunity. She really must make an effort to get on with him better.

'Well, I am grateful for the chance you're giving me,' she said, attempting to inject some warmth into her voice.

'I take it you're enjoying your new position.'

'Yes, I am.'

She did not have to feign her enthusiasm and his eyes were watchful as she described her experiences over the last few weeks.

'Henry's been marvellous,' she concluded, 'but I've learned most by simply throwing myself in at the deep end.'

Rob Hunter looked down at the amber liquid in his glass.

'Tell me, do you ever resent the fact that your family home is now a hotel and full of strangers?'

Tamzin was surprised at the directness of his approach and tried to be equally frank in return.

'I felt resentment at first,' she admitted, 'but I soon realised it was the only way we could stay on here. Of course, things didn't quite work out as Dad had hoped.'

She gazed at the flames as she remembered her father's disappointment when his plans went awry and Thornham House had to be sold.

'And do you resent me, Tamzin, for taking Thornham House away from your family?'

'Certainly not!'

She might resent his arrogant manner but she had no reason to resent his business success!

'As I've already said,' she went on, 'I'm grateful for the opportunity you're giving me, but I am curious on one point.'

'Which is?'

'Why you appointed me at all when you had made it quite clear that you owed my family no favours.'

He glanced down at his glass once more.

'After our first, somewhat stormy meeting, I started thinking about your reaction. It was quite obvious that you had known nothing of your father's activities. I must admit, I had been so incensed by your father's treachery I had, somewhat unfairly, damned all his family by association. I realised after meeting you that that was wrong.'

His eyes rose and held hers.

'To put it bluntly, you made me feel like a heel. I came down here to see if I could make amends and when I saw you on duty and realised you had a natural aptitude for this sort of work, the solution seemed simple.'

Tamzin mulled over his words in

silence, surprise at his humility momentarily robbing her of words. She wondered if this was the right time to tell him of her desire to delve further into what had really happened at Thornham House. She shifted uneasily in her chair when she said, 'I've been thinking over what you told me, quite a lot, recently. I must say I find it difficult to believe in my father's guilt.'

'The facts speak for themselves, Tamzin.'

'But do they?' she persisted. 'I thought I might do a little investigating myself.'

'And how do you propose to do that?'

His voice was ominously quiet.

'Well, if you could give me details of the private detective you hired, I could speak to him and see if there's been some sort of mistake.'

'The only mistake made was telling you what I know!'

Rob Hunter was leaning forward, a harsh light in his eyes. Tamzin shrank back in her chair as his voice continued to harangue her.

'You'll get no information out of me, Tamzin. What I told you was in strict confidence. It would harm my business if it were known that I'd suffered from commercial espionage. I don't want anyone raking over the past, least of all you!'

He glanced down at his watch.

'I'm due to have lunch with your charming sister, now. I'll leave you to finish your sherry in peace.'

He strode to the door, then paused, looking back at her.

'I mean what I say, Tamzin. Don't play girl detective. I won't brook any interference in my affairs.'

The door slammed shut on sudden silence. She'd had no intention of raising Rob Hunter's ire by protesting her father's innocence but if he thought his ugly reaction would deter her he was very much mistaken.

3

Next day, Tamzin learned from Laura that Rob would be staying on for a few more days. She knew, then, that she had to move swiftly if she was to obtain the information she needed before Rob returned to his London office. That afternoon she stabbed out the number of Rob's secretary on her phone in the privacy of the apartment.

'Rob Hunter's office. Who's calling?' the voice replied.

'Jane from Hunter and Davenport,' Tamzin said, naming the firm of auditors who had just carried out an external check on the group's accounts. 'We've one or two loose ends to tidy up,' she added. 'We don't seem to have the details of the detective agency Mr Hunter uses.'

'Really? Well, he always uses Harry Smith's outfit. Just one moment.'

The secretary reeled off a London address and Tamzin thanked her, replacing the receiver. She'd done it! She glanced at the address written on the pad, inwardly congratulating herself.

Now she needed to go to London to speak to this Harry Smith. Arranging cover would be difficult but in that respect Laura might be able to help her. Recently she had begun to do relief work in reception and had demonstrated quite a flair for it. Her free-spirited sister had never really settled down to one line of work since leaving school and Tamzin was keen to encourage her new interest.

Her absence in London would be the perfect excuse for trying Laura out with new responsibilities. It might also have the added benefit of taking her mind off Rob Hunter, Tamzin concluded sourly. Laura was seeing a lot of him during his current stay and Tamzin did not approve at all. He was far too experienced and suave for her younger sister.

Tamzin arranged leave for the following week and Wednesday morning found her taking the earliest train possible. She had to change once and when she reached London took a taxi directly to the address given. Even so, it was mid afternoon by the time she arrived at the office, set amongst a parade of dingy shops.

She pushed open the door to find herself in a small lobby with barely enough room for the large desk piled high with folders. A middle-aged woman peered up at Tamzin over the stack of papers.

'If you're looking for Harry,' she said with a world-weary air, 'he hasn't come back from lunch yet.'

'Perhaps I could wait,' Tamzin suggested.

'As Harry's lunches last all afternoon you might be waiting a long time,' then noting the disappointment on Tamzin's face, she added, 'If you're in a hurry I should go round to the 'Coach and Horses.' '

Tamzin asked for directions and five minutes later found herself pushing open the door into a small bar. It was a small, intimate pub and when she enquired after Harry the bar tender jerked his head in the direction of a man with iron grey hair seated in a far corner, the small, round table before him covered in papers.

'That's Harry, love, doing his office work.'

He looked up at Tamzin's approach.

'Good afternoon, young lady, what may I do for you?' At her surprised look he added, 'I am a private detective, you know. I may have looked as though my nose was stuck to the grindstone but I do know when someone is talking about me.'

Tamzin smiled as she took the seat opposite.

'I see I shall have to be very careful around you, Mr Smith.'

'I'm sure your conscience is clear, Miss . . . ?'

'My name's Tamzin Thornham.'

'Well, Miss Thornham, do you have a job for me?'

'I'm afraid not. I'm here to ask you questions about a job you've done.'

'All the details of my cases are meant to remain secret, client confidentiality and all that. On the other hand . . . ' His face broke into a smile. 'I was never one for sticking to rules. That's why I'm so good at my job. Perhaps you can tell me which case you're interested in and why.'

'My father was Victor Thornham. Rob Hunter told me of his alleged treachery a few weeks ago. As I was working abroad when all this happened it came as a complete surprise to me. I was terribly shocked.'

'I can imagine. I hope you don't blame my investigation for your father's death. I was as sorry as anyone when I heard about his heart attack.'

'No-one is to blame for Dad's death. The post mortem revealed that he had been living on borrowed time. The thing is, Mr Smith, I cannot believe in his guilt. I'd like to ask about your investigation, see if a mistake could have been made.'

'I'm sorry to disappoint you, Miss Thornham, but there could be no mistake. You see your father confessed to me.'

Tamzin's heart sank. She had been hoping against hope that Rob Hunter had got things wrong but now Harry was able to verify what she had been told, first hand.

'But what made you suspect my father in the first place?' she asked.

'Daniel Weston, that's who. When Rob Hunter came to me I had little to go on but I've had a lot of experience in this game and sixth sense told me that Danny Weston was involved somewhere. He's a shrewd operator, Miss Thornham. He started life as a journalist on the city desk for a top broadsheet but soon realised he'd make more money selling the information he gleaned. He soon got the push and set himself up, ostensibly, as a freelance reporter. In reality he continued his

sideline, stealing information for commercial gain.'

'Why hasn't he been arrested and
prosecuted?'

'You need hard evidence and he's
adept at leaving no trace behind. Also,
his victims rarely want to prosecute.
They don't want the rest of the
business world to know they've been
made fools of. Damages their credibility.'

Knowing Rob's sensitivity on the
subject Tamzin did see but she still
didn't know what connection this
Daniel Weston had with her father. She
put this to Harry.

'Well, we put Weston under strict
surveillance. Sure enough he made
several trips to Thornham House. When
I confronted your father he made an
immediate and full confession. And
that's all I can tell you.'

The despair must have shown on her
face.

'Now, now, miss, none of this reflects
on you. You must try to put it behind
you.'

'That's rather difficult,' she said bitterly. 'Perhaps I should speak to this Daniel Weston. I'd like to know why my father succumbed to temptation. Could you give me his address?'

'No way! He's dangerous and unpredictable. I wouldn't dream of letting you near him. As I've already said Miss Thornham, you should return to Devon and get on with your life.'

After this advice it seemed that Harry had nothing more to say and Tamzin took her leave. She had booked into a small, family-run hotel for the night and as she prepared for bed she mulled over the events of the day. It seemed that she would have to admit defeat. However unpalatable the truth was, it seemed that Rob Hunter had been right all along.

Standing on the platform next day, waiting for her train, Tamzin's thoughts strayed once more to her family problems. It was ironic that Rob shared a secret with her denied to her own sister but Tamzin could only be thankful that Laura would be spared the knowledge that she'd disobeyed his instructions and delved further!

'Tamzin! How nice to see you.'

Tamzin's head shot round. No, she had not imagined those familiar, clipped tones. Rob Hunter was standing before her.

'What are you doing here?' she asked, immediately regretting her blunt words.

'Meeting a business friend. I'm sorry I startled you. Are you meeting someone, too? Have I interrupted a liaison?'

'Of course not,' Tamzin said irritably, convinced he enjoyed goading her. 'I'm waiting for my train back to Devon.'

'A journey, I, too, will be making this weekend.'

'You're coming this weekend?'

'Don't look so dismayed, Tamzin. I'm not coming to spy on you. Your charming sister has invited me to a local ball.'

Why did Laura have to be so

54

beautiful? She was drawing Rob Hunter to Devon far more than was necessary. Tamzin supposed she should make some suitable response but as she searched for the right words a tall, blonde woman came up and greeted Rob by kissing him on both cheeks. Rob flashed a smile in Tamzin's direction and then they were gone, strolling away arm in arm. Tamzin watched their retreating backs. Was there no end to the list of Rob Hunter's conquests?

On her return, Tamzin was pleased to find Henry singing Laura's praises, so much so, that he suggested they offer Laura a full-time post as a receptionist.

'It's a humble position to start with,' she told Laura, later, 'but Henry and I will help you and we think you'll be ready to take on extra responsibilities quite soon. So, what do you say?'

'I say you're the best sister in the world!' Laura said and threw her arms around Tamzin, hugging her tight.

When Tamzin disentangled herself,

laughing, she warned Laura that she would have to clear the job offer with Rob.

'I don't want him to think I'm abusing my position by granting favours to relatives.'

'You leave Rob Hunter to me.' Laura's face broke into a smile which, suddenly, made her look years older. 'I'll talk to him about it.'

'You leave all explanations to me,' Tamzin warned, alarmed.

Matters would get very complicated indeed if Laura attempted to use her feminine charms on her behalf.

'Suit yourself,' Laura said, unconcerned. 'Besides, I've to concentrate my energies on choosing a beautiful ball gown for Saturday night.'

She did, indeed, look lovely in the dramatic, full-length gown of black velvet which set off her dark colouring. Tamzin was on duty in reception when she and Rob swept down the staircase, her glamorous appearance matched by Rob's traditional evening suit.

Laura blew Tamzin a kiss as they left and William, who had dropped by to see her, said, 'They certainly make a handsome couple.'

'You're right,' she acknowledged.

'Still worried about the whole thing?' William asked.

'I am,' she admitted. 'I don't trust Rob Hunter where relationships are concerned.'

'But you can trust Laura.'

'William, you know that's not true! She has no sense where men are concerned. She's been flattered continually, never learned to be cautious.'

'Well, never mind Laura,' he said, a shade impatiently. 'Any chance of us having a drink together?'

'I'm afraid not. When I've finished here I have to help out in the restaurant. It'll be hectic all evening. However, you could meet me in the apartment when my shift's over. I really need to talk to you.'

'Sure,' William said, eagerly. 'What time?'

'About eleven. If I'm late, you know where we keep the spare key. Make yourself at home.'

He left and Tamzin continued with her duties, her mind mulling over her decision to talk over with William what she had discovered about her father. Since her return from London she'd been unable to let the matter rest. Doubts remained in spite of Harry's testimony and she hoped that William's counsel might help her to come to terms with her new knowledge. Only then, she reasoned, could she move on as Harry had suggested.

It was past midnight before Tamzin was able to return to the apartment. She supposed, wearily, that William would have given up on her and gone home, but she was wrong. He was on their couch, legs stretched before him, head lolling back on the cushions, fast asleep. Tamzin attempted to tiptoe past but he stirred and sat up, rubbing his eyes.

'Tamzin! I must have dozed off. What time is it?'

'Past midnight, I'm afraid,' she said apologetically. 'We had a really busy evening, quite hectic, in fact. Now, as I've kept you waiting, the least I can do is offer you a night cap. What would you like?'

'Scotch, neat please.'

She poured two measures into tumblers and then joined him on the couch. She would need some Dutch courage, she decided, if she was to confide all to William.

Thankfully, he took the initiative, turning to her with the words, 'You sounded as though you needed to talk earlier, Tamzin, so, go ahead. I'm listening.'

'Thanks,' Tamzin said gratefully. This isn't easy for me so I'll start at the beginning.'

She described her first meeting with Rob Hunter and her investigations so far.

'I seem to have run up against a brick

wall, William. Harry has confirmed Rob Hunter's story and I've no reason to disbelieve either of them, but I still can't accept my father's guilt.'

'I must admit I'm shocked to hear all this. I've known your father for most of my life. I would have sworn by his integrity. We know your father ran into money problems when he first converted the house into a hotel. Perhaps the pressure became intolerable.'

'But he solved those problems by selling out to Rob Hunter,' she pointed out. 'So why jeopardise his newly-found security by cheating?'

'I've no idea, love. There must be something else we don't know.'

'Exactly! That's why I want to speak to this Daniel Weston.'

'No, Tamzin! You mustn't do anything of the kind!'

Tamzin looked at William in surprise. It was unusual for him to be so assertive.

'Weston may be unconvicted but he's

a criminal,' he went on, 'and potentially dangerous. Besides, if you've no care for your own safety remember what type of man he is. He's not likely to tell you the truth.'

'But where does all this leave me?' she went on. 'I feel as though I'm in limbo, unable to accept Dad's guilt but unable to disprove it, either.'

'Look,' he said, his face softening, 'I know you don't want to burden Laura with this, but I know now and I'm willing to give you all the support you need until you can put this behind you and get on with life.'

He drew her towards him and for once she didn't resist, finding it a comfort to feel the warmth of his arms around her as he soothed her with gentle words. Next moment their peace was shattered as the door flew open and Laura practically fell into the room. She regained her balance, then turned to Rob who had followed her in.

'You see,' she said, 'there was no need

to be so quiet. Tamzin and William are still up.'

She waved vaguely in their direction and Tamzin straightened quickly, tidying her hair as Rob scrutinised her, his brows drawn into a very straight line. He'll be accusing me of frolicking on company property tomorrow, she thought, her tension threatening to transmute into nervous giggles. She drew a steadying breath.

'Thank you for bringing Laura home, Mr Hunter, it was very kind of you,' she said.

'Oh, don't be so formal, Tamzin. Rob's come back for coffee. I'll make some for you two as well.'

She began to weave towards the kitchen and William, ignoring the plea in Tamzin's eyes, got up to follow.

'I think I'd better give Laura a helping hand.'

The door closed leaving Rob and Tamzin alone.

'I didn't really want any coffee,' he said, as he seated himself opposite. 'I just wanted to ensure Laura got back to the apartment safely. She is, as you can see, a little merry.'

'Well, she doesn't go to many large functions,' Tamzin said, needled. 'I expect she got carried away.'

'I'm not criticising,' he returned swiftly. 'It's natural to let one's hair down occasionally. After all, Laura is very beautiful, and very young.'

Unlike her spinsterish sister, Tamzin thought inwardly! Rob seemed to think that she was past any sort of social life. There was a distinct air of disapproval about him, at the moment, as though he had discovered her in some flagrant act of misconduct.

'I hope you've had a pleasant evening, Tamzin,' he said, breaking into her troubled thoughts.

'Not as pleasant as yours,' she said drily. 'I was on duty until past midnight.'

'Of course. At least you had company to liven up the end of the shift.'

'It's always pleasant to unwind with a

63

friend,' she said non-committally.

There was an awkward pause and Tamzin, searching feverishly for something to say, came up with the subject of Laura's appointment.

'By the way,' she began, 'I hope you approve of my giving Laura a job in the hotel.'

'Of course I do. Why shouldn't I?'

'Well, she is my sister. I wouldn't want you to think I was handing out undeserved favours to relatives.'

'Nonsense. I expect you to spot talent and act on it.'

In his characteristically abrasive way Rob had put her mind to rest on one topic, but was his endorsement of her sister yet another sign of his growing attachment to Laura? The thought of a serious romance between the two of them filled Tamzin with foreboding.

'And what gloomy thoughts are passing through your mind, may I ask?'

Tamzin, startled by his uncanny ability to define her mood, was searching for a suitable reply, when, thankfully, William entered with a tray of coffee.

'Laura's gone to bed,' he explained. 'She's developed rather a nasty head-ache.'

When Tamzin expressed a wish to go to her sister William dissuaded her.

'I've given her some aspirin, Tamzin. She just needs to sleep now.'

As Tamzin drank the hot coffee she felt exhaustion wash over her. She stifled a yawn and found Rob's watchful gaze on her.

'I'm afraid we're keeping you up, Tamzin.'

He rose, replaced his coffee cup on the table, and said pointedly to William, 'Are you phoning for a taxi or do you have your own car here?'

William returned his challenging stare without flinching.

'Neither, I'm not in need of trans-port.'

Rob Hunter was very still, then a flicker of emotion, difficult to define, fleeted across his face. Tamzin got up and began to tidy up.

'William doesn't need transport,' she said briskly, 'because he lives practically next door and always walks home.'

Rob smiled to reveal white, even teeth.

'How very convenient.'

William sprang to his feet, planted a kiss on Tamzin's cheek and then strolled to the door, saying, 'I expect I'll see you tomorrow, love.'

If Tamzin expected Rob to follow suit she was disappointed. As she carried the dishes into the kitchen he followed, then leaned against the door, watching her as she stacked the dishwasher.

'Will he see you tomorrow?' he asked abruptly, as she finished her task and turned to face him.

'As it's Sunday and my day off I daresay we'll spend the day together. Surely you don't begrudge me time with my friends.'

'Of course not. But young William seems to have the run of the hotel.'

'He has the run of this apartment,'

she corrected him, 'which happens to be my home. And it's very patronising to refer to him as young William,' she added tartly. 'He happens to be the same age as me.'

'You seem much more mature.'

'Thank you!'

Now she felt about a hundred!

'I meant that as a compliment. Don't look daggers at me with those big, green eyes. I happen to be on your side, Tamzin.'

'Are you? Then why are you sneering at my choice of friend?'

'I'm not, although you seem to be very defensive on the subject.'

That smug reply was typical of the man, Tamzin decided, suddenly irate.

'I'm only on the defensive,' she pointed out, 'because I'm constantly subjected to snide innuendo. I may be your employee, Rob, but you don't own my free time. My social life is my business!'

'You've made your point, Tamzin. Now I'll say good-night. No need to see me out.'

Within seconds he was gone, leaving Tamzin to stare at the closed kitchen door. She threw the tea towel down in exasperation and drew shaky fingers through her hair. What on earth had made her overreact like that? She should not have allowed him to goad her into losing her temper.

It must have been weariness which had prompted her to lose her cool, she decided, suddenly fearful of the consequences of alienating the one person who held her future, and Laura's, in the palm of his hand.

4

After her confrontation with Rob, Tamzin hoped to see little of him after his return to London but in that she was disappointed. He visited the hotel most weekends to accompany Laura to various local functions and she seemed to be as starry-eyed about him as ever.

Tamzin kept an uneasy silence on the subject and threw herself even more into work. She contacted her friend Marie in Paris and asked her to look for a suitable agency to work on an account for them. Eventually, Marie came up with the Belmont Agency and Tamzin began to make lengthy phone calls in French to explain exactly what sort of campaign they needed to promote the hotel. After one such phone call, Tamzin replaced the receiver one afternoon and looked up to find Rob entering the room.

'Sorry to disturb you,' he said, 'but I thought Henry was in here.'

'He's just gone down to the kitchens. May I help?'

'Thanks, but it's Henry I need.'

As he turned to go Tamzin called him back.

'Whilst you're here, Rob, perhaps I could have a word.'

'Of course. What's the problem?'

'There's no actual problem. It's just that I've engaged the Belmont Agency in Paris to come up with some proposals to promote the hotel on the Continent. I feel the time has now come to go there in person.'

'To do what, exactly?'

'To scrutinise their ideas, and choose which ones I believe will make the best campaign.'

'That makes perfect sense. When will you go?'

'As soon as I can arrange it with Henry.'

'Plan a visit for two weeks hence, please, Tamzin. Then I'll be able to come with you.'

'You intend to come with me?' Tamzin said, unable to keep the surprise out of her voice.

'Don't sound so dismayed, Tamzin. I have considerably more experience in marketing than you do and as this is such a large undertaking I think you could do with some support.'

She could not argue with this reasoning but why did Rob's offer of support make her feel more nervous, not less?

'It's up to you, of course. You're the boss.'

'I am, aren't I?' he said, his bright tone in marked contrast to her grudging response. 'So when you've sorted out dates, let me know, and I'll organise travel and accommodation.'

William seemed to understand her fears about the trip when she spoke to him and, in his usual down to earth manner, set out to allay them.

'You're looking at this whole thing in the wrong way,' he told her, the day

71

before her departure. 'Rob Hunter has only just appointed you. If you failed it would reflect badly on his judgement. I'm sure he's going with you to ensure your success.'

'I hope you're right.'

William's words made sense and she was to remember them the following day when she met Rob at the airport where they were to take the shuttle to Paris. He looked every inch the formidable businessman that he was. Tamzin only hoped that her fledgling business skills would go some way to matching his over the next few, testing days.

As Rob had been tied up all day they had arranged to take the evening flight. Rob spent most of the time perusing business documents. Just before they were due to land in Paris he slipped the last of them into a slim valise and turned to her with a smile.

'That was the last paper requiring my attention. Now I'm all yours for the next few days.'

As colour tinged her cheeks it was obvious from the hint of amusement in his eyes that her wordless response was all he was seeking. His next words were brisk.

'A car will meet us and take us to the Hotel du Charme. It's one of my favourite hotels, Tamzin. I hope you like it.'

As Tamzin stepped into the foyer, some time later, she declared herself enchanted. The panelled walls were lit by wall lights held in elaborate metal sconces, with stained glass shades which fractured the light across the marbled floor. Large, oval mirrors, hung within recesses, had scenes from Parisian life at the turn of the century etched into the surface.

After registering, the lift, in the form of a wrought-iron cage the colour of old gold, carried them smoothly to the sixth floor. At her door Rob handed her the key.

'I'm next door. Have a rest and freshen up and I'll collect you in one hour for dinner,' he said.

Inside, Tamzin found a small suite of rooms, with ivory antique furniture, dark blue carpeting and soft furnishings in the same colour. The porter had brought up her suitcase and she unpacked swiftly, then showered and slipped into her robe. Seated at the dressing table she brushed her shining hair until it fanned out on to her shoulders. As usual, her skin gleamed translucent, and to add colour she brushed a little blusher on to her high cheekbones. Mascara and a little lip gloss completed her light make-up.

She slipped on her dress and gazed at herself critically in the long, cheval mirror. It was a black straight dress, with shoestring straps. It fitted her like a second skin, and dramatically set off her fair colouring and slim figure. She wound a fine gold chain around her neck and added gold studs to her ears before slipping on patent leather, spiky-heeled shoes. She took one final look at herself in the mirror, and decided her appearance would not disgrace her in whatever fashionable restaurant Rob decided to take her to.

The look on his face as she opened the door to his knock suggested he agreed with her assessment.

'You look very beautiful, Tamzin,' he said softly.

Tamzin knew such compliments tripped easily off his tongue but still found herself flushing with pleasure as she joined him in the corridor.

'Is the restaurant far?' she asked. 'Do I need a coat?'

'No, and no. The restaurant is, in fact, next door.'

They had stopped in front of the door to his room and he flung the door back to reveal a table set for two with a centrepiece of pale pink roses. A trolley, laden with heated dishes, was to one side and a bottle of wine peeped out of an ice bucket on the coffee table. It looked very cosy, and very intimate!

Seeing the doubt shadowing her eyes, he said, 'We've had a very long day. I simply thought you'd prefer to eat in. And this isn't some cheap seduction trick, Tamzin.'

'I know that.'

She went in and sat at the table. She did have qualms about a tête à tête with Rob, but she wasn't going to admit it!

The meal was delicious. Tamzin had wondered what on earth she was going to talk to Rob about but he broke the ice by asking her about her ideas on the proposed marketing campaign. She talked through her views and Rob seemed happy to act as a sounding board for her thoughts, nodding in agreement and contributing only when she needed further encouragement.

He only referred to matters of a more personal nature when they moved on to dessert, a featherlight concoction of chocolate and orange mousse, when he asked her if she had enjoyed her time working in Paris.

'I simply adored it, but I think my thoughts were already turning towards home when I heard about Dad. His death marked the end of an era for me in more ways than one. I have no regrets about returning to Devon.'

'Really? And did you leave no broken-hearted Frenchman behind?'

He flashed her a teasing smile but Tamzin refused to rise to the bait.

'No, I did not.'

'You say that, in your prim, English way, as though you're proud of the fact. Surely Paris is a city made for reckless love affairs.'

'It may be the city of lovers for some,' she said, 'but it wasn't for me.'

'So, you were determined to be faithful to William, the boy next door?'

'William is a friend,' she emphasised, 'a very old and dear one but a friend, nevertheless.'

'I don't think William would like to hear himself described in such terms. According to your sister, he has been in love with you for some years.'

'I'm afraid William mistakes affection for love.'

'You sound very cool, Tamzin. Are

you quite sure there is nothing between you and William except friendship?'

'Yes, I am. The friendship runs deep, but that's all it is.'

'Then why not tell the poor, young man?'

'I do, often,' she protested, 'but William refuses to accept the fact. He continues to hope that one day I'll marry him.'

Her voice trailed away into silence as she realised she had revealed far more than intended. How had he managed to prise such private thoughts from her? Her next words echoed her inner thinking.

'I don't know why I'm telling you all this.'

'Probably because I asked you,' he said tersely. 'I've been unpardonably rude to pry into your private life but I've been curious about you and William for some time.'

Before Tamzin could ask why, there was a knock at the door and then a waiter entered with a large cafetière of coffee. He filled both their cups and then withdrew. They drank in silence, then Rob said, 'I, too, spent several years in Paris, as a student. You can see my old lodgings from here. Come, I'll show you.'

She followed him to the long windows which looked down over the quiet square at the back of the hotel.

'If you crane your head to the left,' he told her, 'you'll see an odd-looking building on the corner with rounded walls, painted in terracotta. I spent two years in an attic room there.'

She was suddenly aware of how close they were and, imperceptibly, began to move away from him.

'Don't draw away from me, Tamzin,' he said sharply. 'Am I so repugnant to you that you don't wish to be near me?'

'No, of course not.'

'Then look at me.'

His hand held her chin, tilting her face so that she was forced to look up into his eyes. She was surprised to see uncertainty there but his next words came as a complete surprise.

'Why do you dislike me so much, Tamzin? Is it because of your father? Do you blame me for his death?'

Tamzin forced her words out through a dry throat.

'I don't blame you, or anyone else for his death, and I don't dislike you.'

That was, strictly speaking, true but she did mistrust him and as his eyes searched her face she attempted to school her features into a neutral mask.

'In spite of what you say,' he said, at last, his words silkily soft, 'there is a barrier between us. Let me see if I can breach it.'

His lips captured hers in a gentle kiss. She intended to draw back but his touch sent her senses reeling and she found herself responding. He groaned, pulling her closer as his mouth grew ever more demanding. Time seemed suspended as Tamzin gave in to the magic of his touch, her heart beating an unsteady rhythm. Control seemed to be spiralling away from her and sudden realisation brought her to her senses. Instinctively, she drew back and he released her, then drew his hands lightly up her bare arms.

'Don't look so shocked, Tamzin. You've hardly behaved like a scarlet woman.'

Yet she felt like one! Her sister was well on the way to being in love with this man and she'd just tumbled into his arms!

'Hey! Look at me. We've done nothing wrong.'

'I know that,' she said, attempting a brittle tone. 'It was just a kiss. It meant nothing.'

A shadow crossed his face.

'Didn't it?'

'Of course not.'

She must leave right now. If she stayed one more moment she would be in danger of succumbing once more to his potent charm.

'I'd better go back to my room. We've a long day ahead of us tomorrow.'

Not waiting for his reply she turned

away but she caught one last glimpse of him as she left the room. Shoulders slightly hunched, he was staring out of the window, his profile forbidding.

That night she tossed and turned, her mind going over and over her searing encounter with Rob. She was profoundly shocked at how easily his touch had breached her defences, arousing a passion in her which she had always recognised his powerful male attractiveness but had naïvely assumed herself immune to it. For one, forlorn moment she wondered if she really knew herself.

At the heart of her disquiet was Laura's obvious infatuation with the man. Although Laura tended to fall in and out of love with predictable regularity she did seem to be harbouring strong feelings for Rob and Tamzin knew she could never do anything to hurt her younger sister.

Besides, if Laura had not been involved, there would still be many objections to a relationship with Rob. It would complicate a professional relationship already fraught because of their differing view on the matter of her father's guilt. Anyway, why would Rob, who seemed to have any number of glamorous women at his beck and call, be interested in a woman such as herself, who did not belong to the high-powered world he inhabited.

No, she was sure the kiss between them had merely been a product of Rob's insatiable desire to flirt with whatever woman he was with. She would be a fool if she allowed her name to join the list of his other conquests.

5

Next morning Tamzin found herself surprisingly refreshed. To her relief Rob did not refer to what had happened the night before and after a hurried breakfast in which work was the sole topic of conversation they took a taxi to the Belmont Agency.

They were introduced to a bewildering number of people and then sat back to watch the presentations. They broke for lunch and in the afternoon it was Tamzin's turn to give her opinion on the ideas they'd been presented with and to ask further questions. Rob seemed happy to take a back seat and she was grateful for his trust as she discussed different approaches with the staff involved. It was decided that they would make a final decision the following day and as they left Tamzin concluded, aloud, that the day had been fruitful.

'I agree,' Rob said. 'The agency seems to have grasped what we are looking for and come up with some exciting proposals.'

'My friend, Marie, told me they were the best. I must thank her when I see her later. Would you like to join us for dinner tonight? I'm sure Marie and Pierre would love to meet you.'

'I thought you'd never ask, Tamzin.'

Marie was equally enthusiastic when Tamzin telephoned her from the hotel to ask if she could bring Rob along.

'Of course, chèrie,' she trilled. 'I am looking forward to seeing the man himself. Pierre will collect you at eight.'

Marie and Pierre lived in an apartment in an elegant eighteenth-century building but had furnished their home with a bright, contemporary look. Later that evening, as Rob looked around appreciatively at the unusual decor Tamzin relaxed, feeling instinctively that the evening would be a success. So it proved. After several hours of lively conversation over delicious food cooked by Marie, Tamzin found herself being congratulated by her friend when she was helping her with the dishes.

'Rob is charming,' she declared. 'I expected a stuffy businessman, but no, he laughs and makes jokes. He praises my home, even my cooking! You must not hesitate, chèrie, you must marry him!'

'Now, hold on, Marie,' Tamzin said, 'Rob's my boss and our relationship's purely professional.'

'You don't make a fool out of me. You two look at each other as though no-one else exists. Yes, it is true. If you are too blind to see it yourself, then I pity you. But think over what I say, or it might be too late for you and Rob.'

Tamzin knew better than to argue with Marie when she was caught up in a romantic flight of fancy but she dismissed her words all the same.

The next morning found them back at the agency. A good night's sleep had clarified Tamzin's thinking and they were able to finalise details for the new campaign without too much difficulty. Reluctant to let his valued new clients go, the director of the agency asked them out to lunch and they found themselves whisked off to a well-known restaurant in central Paris.

The meal lasted well into the afternoon and by the time they returned to the hotel Tamzin had developed a thumping headache. She made her excuses to Rob and went straight up to her room to lie down. She fell into a deep sleep, waking up with a start some hours later. Her headache was gone but she felt the need to freshen up. Before she showered, she rang down and ordered coffee. The hot shower revived her sluggish senses and as she was drying herself she heard a knock at the door. Assuming it to be the waiter she called through for him to enter, then slipped on her robe. Returning to the sitting-room she stopped short at the sight of Rob pouring coffee into two cups.

'I slipped in with the waiter,' he said, handing her a cup. 'I hope you don't mind but I wanted to see how you were.'

Tamzin did mind his presence but, realising it would be churlish to say so, contented herself with, 'My headache has quite disappeared. I'm afraid I over-indulged at lunch.'

'I suppose this rules out supper.'

'I'm afraid so. I'm going to read for a while and then have an early night. We have a lot of travelling to do tomorrow.'

'Yes, we do,' he repeated absently, looking around the room.

When is he going to go, she wondered impatiently. She yawned, a little ostentatiously, replacing her cup on the tray as he moved to her side.

'I'm sorry, I'm keeping you up when, obviously, you wish to see the back of me,' he said.

'It's just that I'm rather tired,' Tamzin said.

'No need to make excuses, Tamzin. I

know you find my company tiresome.'

'It's not like that at all,' she protested.

She felt tense around him, true, but she had never disliked his company.

'Look, these past two days have been very enjoyable for me but very stressful. I've had to prove myself in an area I've had little experience in, in front of you, my boss, and some pretty sophisticated advertising executives. This hasn't been a holiday, Rob, and I've little energy left to play charming companion.'

He laid one finger on her lips, saying, 'You've made your point. You've been under pressure and I've been my usual, insensitive self.'

He smiled down at her, the look in his eyes taking away the sting of his words. He cradled her face gently in his hands, his eyes coming to rest on her moistened eyes. What he saw there caused his head to dip and as his lips met hers she clung to him as though to steady herself, helpless for the moment to resist the powerful feelings sweeping through her.

At last his lips broke from hers.

'I suppose I should apologise for that, Tamzin, but you didn't fake your response. Does this mean you do have some feelings for me?'

'Whatever I may be feeling,' she said cautiously, 'I still don't think I should be in your arms.'

'Why not?' he said, frowning. 'You told me last night that you weren't committed to William. Is there someone else you haven't told me about?'

'Of course not,' she replied. 'It's not me who's attached, it's you!'

'I am? Who is the lucky lady supposed to be?'

'Laura, of course, my sister!'

Realisation dawned on his face.

'You think I'm in love with her?'

'It's a natural assumption. You visit her most weekends.'

'You goose. I've been visiting in the hope of getting close to you!'

Tamzin could barely take in the words she was hearing. At last she said, 'I don't understand this, Rob. You and

Laura seemed so close.'

'We are, as friends. We swim and play tennis together, and I spend all my time asking her about you! Don't get me wrong. I think Laura's a real nice kid but I spent time with Laura because you placed barrier after barrier between us and I just couldn't get close. Laura has never interested me as a woman in the way you do.'

Tamzin sensed that the admission cost him dear but she knew she could not give him the response he was seeking. She broke the tense silence.

'I'm feeling totally confused, Rob. Up to this moment I thought you were involved with Laura and I've never considered the possibility of anything between the two of us. I simply don't know how to react.'

'Follow your instincts,' he urged her. 'Haven't you just revealed your feelings by the way you responded to my kiss?'

'Perhaps. I need time to think things through,' she added, 'and I need time to speak to Laura. She might view your relationship in a different light and I want to know how she feels about you.'

'You do that. I'm sure you'll find that she's not in love with me. Then, perhaps, you'll give me a chance to show you what you and I could mean to each other.'

He planted a kiss on her forehead.

'With this chaste kiss I'll bid you good-night. You and I part company tomorrow and I'll give you the time you're seeking. But, please, Tamzin, don't keep me waiting for too long.'

Then he was gone. Tamzin touched her mouth gingerly with her fingers, shivering as she remembered the feel of his lips. She had no intention of being bounced into a relationship with Rob but, in the end, would she have any choice but to give in to the powerful feelings he aroused?

After the eventful Paris trip, Tamzin came to earth with a crunch when she found Thornham House in the grip of a flu epidemic which had decimated the staff. She had to work long hours to cover for absent staff and when Laura took ill she had to nurse her sister as well. Under the circumstances she had little time to consider what had happened between herself and Rob and when she did the whole thing seemed like a distant dream.

On her return from Paris she had found herself reluctant to broach the subject with Laura and when she took ill, Tamzin realised, guiltily, that she was relieved that she now had an excuse not to speak. She had no contact with Rob following her return and was grateful that he had honoured his promise not to pressurise her. The problem still remained, though. She was still unsure of her feelings and very wary of his intentions towards her.

Laura recovered, although she still seemed listless and out of sorts, and the epidemic abated, leaving Tamzin with an easier work load. Now she had no excuse for putting off decisions and knew that she needed to speak frankly with her sister. One morning, when they were enjoying an extended coffee break, Tamzin took her courage in both hands.

'I've been waiting for a quiet moment to ask you something, Laura.'

Laura put down her cup, looking across at her sister.

'It's rather a delicate matter,' Tamzin went on. 'It concerns your relationship with, well, with — '

'Are you going to ask me about a boyfriend?'

Laura's eyes were bright, sudden colour etching her cheek.

'In a way,' Tamzin said cautiously.

'Then, don't. I don't want to speak about men. I'm surprised you should ask me, anyway. You know it's none of your business.'

She stood up, pushing her chair back so roughly it almost fell over.

'I didn't mean to upset you,' Tamzin said, trying to salvage the conversation.

'You didn't. It's just that parts of my life are off bounds, even to you.'

She hurried off without a backward

glance leaving Tamzin to stare after her in consternation. Why had Laura reacted so testily? Had she guessed what she had been about to say? As far as she was aware there was no other man on the scene so Laura must have assumed she was about to talk about Rob. Tamzin could only conclude miserably that Laura did care for Rob and felt too deeply to express her feelings openly, even to her sister.

Over the next few days, Tamzin couldn't help but feel that Laura was avoiding her. She volunteered for any overtime that was going and when she had free time spent most of it away from the apartment. When Saturday came, and they were both off work, Tamzin was relieved when Laura said she intended to spend the day with Jane, an old school friend. At least she would be spared her sister's strange mood, deciding to have a quiet day catching up on some reading. Her plans were put on hold, however, when Henry asked her to see one of their suppliers to negotiate a new contract and mid-morning found her battling with traffic on the road to Exeter.

The negotiations went surprisingly well and she found herself free for lunchtime. The thought of going back to Thornham House did not appeal and she decided to spend the rest of the afternoon shopping and having her hair done. By late afternoon she was ready for some tea and set off for the Grand Hotel, a favourite of hers and Laura's whenever they were in town.

Just as she was about to cross the road to reach the entrance, to her surprise, Laura emerged. She and Jane must have decided to treat themselves to tea out as well, Tamzin thought, automatically waving and shouting out her sister's name. A coach passed in front of her, blocking Laura from view, the noise of the engine drowning out her words.

When the vehicle passed, she was just about to shout again when the words died on her lips as her eyes took in the tall figure of Rob Hunter standing beside Laura, one arm solicitously around her shoulders. Rob must have been her companion in the hotel, but why hadn't Laura said she was meeting him today? Why had she lied about spending the day with Jane?

Tamzin shrank back as a crowd of chattering American tourists enveloped her, camouflaging her from view, not that she was in imminent danger of being seen. Rob and Laura had eyes for no-one but each other, heads close together. Next moment Rob's car and driver drew up and they climbed in, and were gone.

Tamzin stood stock still for a few moments, trying to figure out what she had just seen. She couldn't understand why Laura had been deceitful. Her sister was unaware of the attraction that had flared between herself and Rob in Paris, so why not openly admit to be seeing him? Was she being manipulated by Rob for some reason known only to himself? Was he trying to play the sisters off against each other? Tamzin shook her head, aware that she was allowing her imagination to run away with her. Only Laura could explain her actions and Tamzin determined to ask her as soon as she saw her that evening. In the meantime, she crossed the road and went into the Grand Hotel.

It was early evening as she drove into the carpark at Thornham House and as she drew to a halt she saw the sleek lines of Rob's car parked in one of the spaces reserved for staff. Deciding that she could not avoid him and Laura for ever she got out of the car and hurried into Reception. Rob and Laura were standing just inside the door, and to her embarrassment, she almost cannoned into them.

They drew apart abruptly, Laura turning to Tamzin with, 'Tamzin! Rob's come to see us! Isn't that nice? Luckily, he was on hand when I needed a lift. Jane dropped me at the crossroads and I was all set to walk back when Rob came by.'

'I thought it was about time I visited Thornham House again,' Rob added, 'so I decided to come on the spur of the moment. I hope you don't mind.'

'Of course not,' Tamzin said. 'I hope you had a good journey down from London,' she added pointedly.

'It was fine,' Rob returned.

Tamzin opened her mouth and then closed it again. Obviously he was not going to tell her of his detour to Exeter and she could hardly accuse her sister and her boss of playing some sort of a sneaky game while they stood in a crowded reception full of guests.

'Rob! This is an unexpected pleasure.'

Tamzin turned to find Henry at their side.

'I've been trying to get you on the phone for the last two days,' he told Rob, 'so your arrival is very fortuitous. Could you spare a few moments?'

Rob allowed himself to be led off, leaving the sisters alone. Now, perhaps Tamzin could get some answers but as she turned to Laura she headed for the stairs, saying, 'Time to freshen up, I think.'

Tamzin set off in pursuit and reached the apartment just after Laura, slamming the door shut behind her.

'Before you go and shower,' she said, 'I'd just like to ask you something.'

'What is it?' Laura said absently, rummaging in her handbag.

'Well, I was in Exeter today.'

'Really? I thought you were going to have a quiet day in,' Laura replied.

'Henry asked me to go there on business, but never mind me,' she said impatiently. 'The thing is I saw you there.'

'Don't be ridiculous!'

She had all of Laura's attention now.

'I spent the day with Jane. You know I did.'

'All I know is that I saw you in Exeter.'

'You saw someone who looked like me. Really, Tamzin, I don't know what's come over you. You've been in a strange mood ever since you came back from

Paris. I've no time to talk now, I'm desperate for a shower.'

She swept out of the room, leaving Tamzin fuming. Laura had just lied blatantly, and contradicted her to her face! Tamzin knew her sister's stubborn moods all too well. She would have no chance of finding out the truth now. She considered confronting Rob and then dismissed the idea. He had shown his willing complicity by backing Laura up. He would be no more forthcoming than she was and the only purpose she would serve would be to antagonise her boss and possibly damage her own career. Let Rob and Laura have their little secrets, she decided. If they wanted to keep her in the dark, so be it.

Throughout the evening, her mood did not improve. Laura went out and she attempted to relax in front of the television but her mind kept wandering to her current problems. The fact was that she found Laura's baffling behaviour deeply hurtful. They had always been so close, so why was she now shutting her out? Was it some evil influence on Rob's part? Their troubles seemed to stem from when he had entered their lives. To think she had almost succumbed to his charm herself!

She shivered inwardly at the thought of how he had aroused deep emotions within her only a short time ago. Thank goodness she had discovered his deceitful nature before it had been too late.

The ringing doorbell broke into her thoughts and when she opened the door to find Rob there she had difficulty in concealing her surprise.

'Laura's not here, Rob, if you're looking for her.'

'I'm not. I've come to see you. Are you going to ask me in?'

Tamzin let him into the hallway but made no attempt to take him through into the lounge.

'Are we to stand in the passageway, Tamzin?'

'I'm rather tired,' Tamzin said stiffly. 'I was going to have an early night.'

'I see. Well, I won't take up much of

your time, Tamzin. Only I haven't heard from you since we returned from Paris, and there was some unfinished business between us.'

Surely he wasn't attempting to resurrect the notion that there could be anything romantic between them. It was time she put him straight.

'I don't think so, Rob. I think we both got a little carried away. Paris is, after all, a very magical city. On reflection, I'm sure you'll agree that we are better keeping our relationship on a purely professional footing.'

'That's not the impression you gave me in Paris, Tamzin.'

'I'm sorry if I gave you the wrong impression,' she said, attempting a conciliatory tone, 'but I want things to be absolutely clear between us now. After all, we do have to work together.'

For one moment she thought he was going to argue further, then he said, 'If that's what you want, I'll respect your wishes. Good-night.'

Within seconds he was gone and

Tamzin leaned against the closed door, breathing a sigh of relief. One thing this whole unpleasant business had done was clarify her feelings towards Rob. She could never feel deeply towards someone who seemed to be playing off her sister against her. She may never get to the bottom of his double-dealing but at least she hadn't entrusted him with her heart.

6

Tamzin thought she would feel greatly relieved now that things were resolved between herself and Rob, but instead she felt strangely bereft as though something had been taken from her. There was also the thorny problem of her strained relationship with Laura but her sister made it abundantly clear that she was unwilling to re-open the topic of her whereabouts the previous Saturday.

When William telephoned and asked her over to dinner one evening she agreed readily, happy to escape the increasingly fraught atmosphere at Thornham House. As they ate Tamzin brought William up to date with all that had been happening at the hotel, concentrating on the effects of the flu epidemic and leaving out her problems with Laura entirely.

'I heard all about the epidemic on the grapevine,' he told her, 'so I wasn't surprised when you didn't get in touch on your return from Paris.'

'It has been hectic,' she confessed, 'but I should have got in touch. I'm sorry.'

'Well, you're here now, and it's lovely to see you.'

'The feeling's mutual,' Tamzin said and meant it.

After the emotional buffeting of the last few weeks it was soothing to find herself in William's easy company. They finished eating and then Tamzin went through to the lounge. When William brought a tray of coffee in he placed it on the low table and then joined her on the sofa, turning to her.

'You know, Tamzin, I've really missed you these last few weeks. I thought we were becoming quite close before you went off to Paris.'

She realised the truth of his words as he spoke. Since she had taken on her demanding rôle as manager, he had provided her with much support.

'I don't think I realised just how much your help has meant to me, until recently,' she admitted candidly.

She suddenly felt grateful for William's steady qualities. She couldn't imagine him going in for the sort of double dealing that seemed second nature to Rob Hunter! When he took her hand in his she didn't withdraw it.

'I know I've broached this before, Tamzin, but do you think I could ever be more to you than a friend? Is there any chance you could ever marry me?'

Tamzin had deflected this question before but now the audacious thought crept into her mind — why not? Why not give William the answer he richly deserved?

'Would it make you truly happy to marry me?' she asked, shakily.

'Of course it would, darling.'

'Then I'll marry you,' she found herself saying, 'and I promise you I'll do my best to make you a good wife.'

The rest of the evening passed in a

whirl of champagne and crazy conversation in which William planned their honeymoon and then their future life together. He seemed quite happy with her responses and when he kissed her good-night he arranged to spend the following day with her.

Tamzin did not see Laura before she tumbled into bed and, in spite of all that happened, fell into a deep slumber.

Next day she woke to the startling knowledge that she was to be William's bride! Immediately doubts assailed her. Did she love William enough, and in the right way? Next moment her natural good sense asserted itself. She had known William too long to be swept away by some crazy passion but there was nothing inferior in the deep affection she felt for him and many happy marriages had been built on far less.

When she opened the door to him later and saw the happiness on his face this was a further reassurance that she had made the right decision.

'What did Laura say when you told her?' he asked.

'That's a moot point. She was already in bed when I got in last night and she's nowhere to be seen this morning.'

'Well, let's go and find her. She must be somewhere in the hotel.'

He caught her hand and they set off. The receptionist pointed them in the direction of one of the small lounges and when they entered they found it empty, save for a couple by the window, heads close together. Laura and Rob! They broke apart as Tamzin and William approached, and, without pre-amble William burst out his news.

'Wonderful news, folks! Tamzin's agreed to marry me!'

Laura squealed and threw herself upon her sister. As Tamzin disentangled herself from her embrace she caught sight of Rob's face for the first time and her breath caught in her throat at what she saw there. His face was rigid with barely concealed anger and his voice icily polite when he said, 'I suppose congratulations are in order.'

'Thank you,' Tamzin said stiffly.

She had no idea why he was behaving so strangely. She was perfectly free to make her own decisions and certainly did not need his approval. As they left the room Tamzin had the uncomfortable feeling that hostile eyes followed their every move. She and William spent the rest of the day at the coast but when William dropped her back home, early evening, she decided against going back to the apartment. Laura would be there, doubtless with Rob, and she was in no mood to play gooseberry. The night was now drawing in so Tamzin fetched her small torch from her car, fastened up her jacket, and set off down the path which led through the market garden into the open parkland.

She hunched her shoulders against the prevailing wind, her way picked out by the narrow beam of the torch, when a cry caused her to stop. She looked back to see a tall figure behind her, his words lost on the wind. Rob!

He appeared to be gaining ground on her and without thinking, Tamzin set off at a jog, heading for the small copse to her right. Although she could find her way blindfolded she doubted Rob could. As the trees enfolded her, and she moved farther into the wood, she felt sure that she had shaken Rob off. She climbed over a stile, then began to negotiate her way out of the wood. She knew there was a gap in the hawthorn hedge which marked the edge of the wood and hoped her sense of direction had not deserted her. To her relief a break in the hedge loomed before her and she was just about to scramble through when she heard a voice.

'Need a hand?'

Instinctively she reached for the hand on offer and next moment found herself being hauled through the gap.

'How did you get here?' she snapped.

'When I saw you haring into the woods I cut across the parkland to head you off. I knew you had to exit about here and, in spite of your efforts to avoid me, I was determined to speak to you.'

'About what?'

'About your engagement, of course.'

He seized her right shoulder with his hand and pulled her round so that she had no choice but to meet his eyes.

'I don't think any explanation is necessary,' she said. 'William and I have known each other for years and have much in common. It's quite natural that we should wish to marry.'

'It's quite unnatural. You don't love him.'

'Of course I do!'

'Well, that's not what you said in Paris.'

'I've since realised I made a mistake in saying that. Surely I'm entitled to change my mind.'

'A woman's prerogative?' Rob sneered. 'You seemed to have changed your mind about a lot of things since we were in Paris together. Your behaviour towards me has been rather inconsistent, to say the least.'

Tamzin bit back the angry retort that sprang to her lips. If she had learned one thing in her dealings with Rob it was that it was preferable to keep a cool head.

'I've already told you, Rob, I'm really sorry if I gave you the wrong impression when we were abroad. I do value your friendship, but — '

'Spare me the words of comfort, Tamzin. I've no intention of pressing my suit further but I would like to know why you're throwing yourself away on a man not worthy of you.'

'William is worth ten of me,' she snapped, 'and I'll thank you not to criticise him or my decision to marry him. It really is none of your business.'

'Isn't it? Can you look me in the eye and tell me that you love William with all your heart?'

He gripped her chin, tilting her head so that she had no choice but to face the full force of his dark, probing eyes. She felt as though he was looking into

113

her inner self, discovering what was hidden deep within her. She blinked, attempting to break the spell, somehow finding the strength to say, 'I do love William and I've every intention of making him a good wife.'

'Then I wish you and William joy of each other.'

Next moment he was gone and Tamzin was left alone in the dark. She hugged herself as a sharp wind cut through her. What was she to make of his strange behaviour? He was annoyingly adept at making her feel as though she was in the wrong. She had found herself having to defend her decision to marry William when she knew she had done nothing wrong or dishonourable. She would never fathom the man!

To her relief, Rob returned to London the following day. Laura seemed unconcerned and announced that she would be going to London when she next had free time and would see him then. This set the pattern for the next few weeks. They saw nothing of Rob at the hotel but Laura made frequent trips to the capital and, although she remained reticent, Tamzin could only assume that their relationship was proceeding apace.

Tamzin's thoughts and energies were increasingly monopolised by preparations for Christmas at the hotel. William was understanding when she explained that their wedding plans must be put on hold until after the festive season.

After the holiday period, Tamzin had her professional reward for all her hard work when Henry called her in to the office one morning.

'A preliminary look shows a substantial increase in our profits over the same time last year,' he told her, flashing up the results on the computer screen. 'More to the point, the guests seemed to have really enjoyed themselves. We've already had some bookings for next year. Much of it's down to you, Tamzin. Well done.'

Gratified as she was by this praise, the end of the Christmas rush brought a hiatus which was echoed in her personal life. Her engagement to William still did not seem quite real and she knew he was waiting patiently for her to set a date. For both their sakes she had to make a decision.

'You know,' she said to him one afternoon, 'I've always wanted to be a June bride. If we smooth-talk the vicar do you think he'll find a date for us in his busy calendar?'

'Leave it to me. He's been expecting us to marry for years. He'll fit us in!'

Now that they had made such a commitment Tamzin would have loved to have talked through her plans with Laura but her sister remained increasingly distant. Tamzin often wondered forlornly if she had done something, unwittingly, to offend her sister and drive her away from her.

One afternoon she was at the village pub, discussing a drinks order with the landlord, when, as if on cue, a fair-haired stocky man ran down the stairs and into the residents' lounge. It was the man she had seen, months before, with Laura. She had never asked her sister about her date that night and turned to the landlord with an enquiring smile.

'I've seen that chap here before. He's a Londoner, isn't he?'

'Mr Weston? Pure Cockney, I should imagine. He visits here from time to time. He's a good customer, always free with his tips.'

The sound of his name reverberated through Tamzin's mind.

'His first name isn't Daniel, is it?'

'Yes! Dan Weston. Do you know him?'

'Only by reputation.'

She glanced across at the closed door to the lounge. It was difficult to believe that the man who had snared her father was sitting a few feet from her, unaware of her presence. She had to steel herself not to burst into the room and confront him. She knew she needed time to think and left the pub, heading for the coast. She found a headland, deserted on this cold, January afternoon and parked the car. She stared unseeingly at the wintry view.

At one time she had been desperate to track down Weston and question him on his dealings with her father. Now he was sitting in a room in her very own local but the whole thing was complicated by the fact that, somewhere, Laura was involved. She had seen them together with her own eyes. Why hadn't she asked Laura about him after she'd seen them together?

If Weston was intending to target her sister in the same way as he'd targeted her father, she could have stalled him. If he was back in the area he must be here to see Laura again, but this time she would be ready for him!

She glanced at her watch. She must get back before Laura finished her shift on Reception. She would talk to her and find out exactly how far her involvement with Weston had gone before revealing what a snake in the grass he was. It would mean telling Laura about their father but perhaps it was time that she knew the truth.

She returned to the hotel, to be confronted with Henry in Reception.

'Where's Laura? I thought she was supposed to be on duty.'

'She was until about half an hour ago,' Henry replied. 'She had an appointment and asked me to cover here for her.'

The appointment was no doubt with Daniel Weston! Without a word Tamzin retraced her steps back to her car and headed for the pub. As she walked towards the entrance she glanced at the lighted windows of the small lounge. In a replay of what she had seen before, Laura and Weston were in the same corner, huddled together. Fury rose within her. Wasn't Weston content to ruin one member of her family? Was he now determined to ruin Laura as well?

Without pausing to think, she hurried inside and then pushed open the door into the lounge. Laura barely had time to register surprise before she was upon her.

'I want to speak to you right now, Laura,' Tamzin said. 'And I want no excuses.'

'Tamzin!'

Shock fleeted across Laura's features, then she rose, and leaned across to Daniel Weston.

'Sorry about all the drama. Some family crisis to sort out. Back in a moment, darling.'

As Tamzin looked on indignantly, Weston shot a bemused look in her direction and shrugged wide shoulders. Next moment Laura was hurrying her from the room.

'What on earth do you think you're doing? Go away and stay away, Tamzin. You'll ruin everything!'

Tamzin was shocked speechless. Laura had never spoken to her like that before! With one last warning glance her sister disappeared back into the room and Tamzin was left alone.

'Do what she says, Tamzin,' came a familiar voice.

She whipped round to find Rob in front of her, a warning finger held to his lips. Then he beckoned for her to follow and, biting back the questions that rose to her lips, she complied, following him up the stairs to the first floor. He stopped in front of a door and when she caught up with him drew her inside the empty bedroom.

'Rob, what on earth's going on? Why is Laura downstairs with that horrible man? She's not safe, you've to get her away.'

'I promise you that Laura is quite safe and that all your questions will be answered shortly. In return you must promise to stay here and not to interfere. Do you agree?'

It was quite clear from his tone that Rob was in no mood for argument. She nodded, in silent agreement, and then he was gone, leaving her alone. She seated herself on the bed, wondering how long she would have to wait before Rob returned.

7

It seemed like an age before the sound of an engine drew Tamzin to the window. Daniel Weston's car was just leaving the carpark and from this angle she could see quite clearly that he was alone! With relief Tamzin turned round only to find Rob and Laura entering the room. Laura took one look at her sister's face then turned to Rob.

'Could you leave us, please, Rob? I need to speak to Tamzin alone.'

He left with demur, then Laura held up one hand warningly.

'I know you have a lot of questions, Tamzin, but, please, just sit down and listen.'

Tamzin did as she was asked. As Laura drew up a chair Tamzin was struck by how pale and wan she looked. She seemed to have lost weight over these last weeks. Perhaps now she would finally find out what was the cause of her sister's strange behaviour.

'I'm going to begin with the most difficult part,' Laura said suddenly. 'It was me who passed commercial information on to Daniel Weston, not Dad.'

'Oh, Laura!' she exclaimed thinking how she had set out to shelter Laura from what had happened! 'So Dad confessed to protect you?'

'Yes, although I'd no idea at the time. I only found out about his confession recently.'

'I can hardly take in what you're saying. Tell me what happened from the very beginning. How did you meet someone like Weston?'

'He met me,' she said drily. 'We had a 'chance' encounter in the village pub one night and it went on from there. He knows how to charm gullible, young women well enough. Also he was very different from the people I was used to meeting. Before too long I was convinced I was head over heels in love with him.'

'But didn't Dad object to you dating such a man?'

'Dad didn't know. He was too busy running the hotel to wonder where I went at night and I still had enough sense not to parade Daniel in front of him. You, of course, were in Paris, so there was nothing to stop the relationship from developing.'

'But how did he persuade you to pass on information?'

'You're forgetting how clever Daniel Weston is. I'm sure he realised I would never, knowingly, steal information so he decided on a different approach. He told me that he was starting up a business, in hotel supplies, and it would help him no end if he had more information on the Hunter group. Like a fool, I fed him what he asked for. It looked like gobbledegook to me. I swear to you, Tamzin, I'd no idea I was passing on sensitive information.'

Tamzin could well believe it. Laura had always had a tendency to let her heart rule her head.

'How did Dad find out?' Tamzin asked.

'He caught me faxing documents, and soon got the whole story out of me. He'd heard of Daniel by reputation and soon put me straight as to his real intentions. Honestly, Tamzin, I've never seen him so angry. He insisted I pack immediately and go straight to you in Paris. I did as I was told, and I never saw him alive again.'

Her voice broke on a sob but when Tamzin leaned forward to comfort her she pulled back.

'I'll be all right in a minute, really, I will. I don't want to break off now. I need to tell you everything. You see, when I arrived at your place in Paris I thought the whole matter was closed. I knew I'd been a damned fool but thought no-one would ever know, save me and Dad. I lived in ignorance of Dad's confession until Daniel Weston came back into my life.'

'And when was that?'

'He made contact shortly after you

126

became manager. I daresay he thought I'd be in a position to help him again. He tried to smooth-talk me round but I made it clear I didn't want anything to do with him. And I thought that was that.'

'Then what happened?'

'He contacted me again when you and Rob were in Paris. Somehow he'd found out about Dad's confession and when he told me I was completely devastated. Then he threatened to tell Rob the truth if I didn't help him further, reminding me that your career would be on the line as well as our home if Rob discovered it had been me who had betrayed him.'

'Laura, you didn't give into his blackmail, did you?'

'Of course not. I was in a terrible state, but I knew I could never give in to his demands, so I went to Rob and confessed everything.'

'That took a lot of courage, love.'

'It was the least I could do after all the damage my actions had caused.'

'How did he respond?'

'Remarkably well. He knows how manipulative Weston can be and accepted my explanation that I was duped into helping him. I told Rob I was prepared to face the consequences of what I had done and make a full statement to the police.'

'And did you?'

'I did. Rob went with me and they were very interested in what I had to say. They've been trying to get something on Weston for a very long time but Chief Inspector Morris, who dealt with me, wasn't at all sure that my evidence would be enough so he asked me if I'd co-operate in an undercover operation to trap Weston once and for all.'

'That's why you were with Weston just now?' Tamzin asked.

'Yes, and that was our fourth, and hopefully final, meeting. Each time, I've been wired, with the police installed in a surveillance van close by. I've passed over dummy documents and discussed payment with the aim of obtaining enough evidence to bury the man in court.'

'And I've just walked in on you!' Tamzin groaned. 'What on earth did he think? Did it ruin everything?'

'I don't think so. I think I convinced him it was just a family spat.'

'It could have been avoided if you'd told me what was happening.'

'Tamzin, I was so ashamed of what I'd done, especially when I knew about Dad, that I wanted to make amends before telling you the truth. I didn't want you to hate me.'

'You goose. I could never hate you.'

She moved across to her sister and put an arm around her.

'But, darling, what you did was very brave. Weren't you afraid?'

'Not really. I knew the police were listening in and Rob's been keeping a watchful eye on me. He acted as liaison between me and the police.'

'I thought you two shared a secret,' Tamzin said.

'When you saw me in Exeter that time I was meeting Rob to discuss tactics. When you tackled me about it I panicked and, stupidly, denied I'd ever been there. I suppose I just made you more suspicious.'

'Your behaviour puzzled me, certainly, but I never came close to guessing the truth.'

There was a knock at the door and then it opened to admit a tall, thin grey-haired man, closely followed by Rob. The newcomer introduced himself as Chief Inspector Morris. Tamzin rose to take the hand offered.

'I must apologise for breaking in on Laura like that.'

'You weren't to know, Miss Thornham, and it doesn't seem to have done any harm. Laura handled it very well.'

He flashed a smile in her direction.

'Many thanks for your help, my dear. We've enough evidence to pull Weston in now. We've man waiting at his London flat. We'll arrest him as soon as he gets home. Now, if you'd like to come with me we'll divest you of the surveillance equipment, then take you home.'

He ushered Laura out, leaving Rob and Tamzin alone. Rob's eyes took in Tamzin's pale features and he said brusquely, 'You look terrible. Why don't you sit down?'

'I'm all right. I — '

She swayed and next moment strong arms were around her and she was being led to the bed. She sat down, putting her head in her hands, and when a glass was placed in her hand she drank down the fiery liquid, her senses steadying abruptly.

'Phew,' she said, rubbing her forehead, 'that was certainly effective, whatever it was!'

'Neat whisky,' Rob admitted. 'It looks as though all this has come as a great shock to you.'

'It has. I've been kept in the dark about so many things.'

'I'm sorry I had to keep quiet but Laura swore me to secrecy.'

131

'Oh, I don't blame you and I understand Laura's point of view, but when I think of the risks she took, I just . . . '

She shuddered and next moment his arms tightened around her and she was pulled against him, one hand stroking her hair as he soothed her with gentle words. She could feel the strong beat of his heart and as her trembling subsided could only marvel at how safe she felt in his arms. Then, suddenly remembering William, she pulled away.

'I'm sorry. I'm behaving like a Victorian miss. You must be heartily sick of the Thornham family and its problems.'

'Nonsense.'

He stood up, offering his hand.

'I'll drive you back in your car, Tamzin. You're in no fit state to drive.'

'But what about yours?'

'I came here with the police. They're fussing over Laura now and have quite forgotten me. When we get back to the hotel I'll get Henry to rustle up a room for me. It's too late to return to London now.'

They were quiet on the journey back but as they turned in at the hotel gates Rob said, 'One thing puzzles me, Tamzin. From your reaction to seeing Weston and Laura together you clearly knew the danger he represented. But how? When I told you about your father I never mentioned Weston.'

He drew the car to a halt, switched off the engine and turned to her with a wry smile.

'Do you have anything to confess, Tamzin?'

'I'm afraid so,' and Tamzin relayed what had happened when she'd seen Harry Smith, concluding with, 'So I'm sorry I disobeyed your instructions to stay out of this.'

'I doubt that. It was quite wrong of me to try to stop you in the first place. And you were right all along. Your father was innocent.'

'But my sister wasn't,' Tamzin sighed.

'Don't be too hard on her, Tamzin.

She was foolish, not dishonest, and she's paid her dues now.'

'I know and I think your support has helped a lot. Thank you for that.'

'I played only a small part, Tamzin. Weston's downfall can be attributed solely to Laura's courage and determination. I think you can be very proud of your little sister.'

They got out and hurried into the lobby. Just as they were about to part Tamzin remembered that she was seeing William the next day. She detained Rob with one hand on his arm.

'Am I free to tell William everything that has happened? He'll be part of the family soon. I'd hate to keep anything from him.'

Rob's face tightened fractionally.

'I don't see why not, as long as Laura has no objections.'

When she discussed it with her sister, later, Laura agreed, with one surprising condition.

'I'd like to tell William myself,' she

said. 'I've known William all my life and I'd hate him to think badly of me.'

When William arrived the following afternoon he found both sisters waiting for him. He listened to Laura in silence and then his response was all that Laura could have hoped.

'You poor love! What a terrible time you've had!'

Next moment he was hugging her fiercely and Tamzin crept out of the room. Laura needs a hug, she thought. It occurred to her suddenly that she had not considered one aspect of the revelations at all. Rob and Laura were, clearly, not romantically linked. They had been thrown together by events but now everything was out in the open Tamzin could see, for the first time, that they were friends, and nothing more.

Would she have got engaged to William if she had known that? She brushed away the disloyal thought. She couldn't change the past now. The fact was she was engaged to William and he was a wonderful man who deserved her undivided loyalty. She had no intention of letting him down.

Her thoughts were interrupted by a knock at the door. As soon as Tamzin opened the door and found Chief Inspector Morris standing before her, grim-faced, she knew there was something terribly wrong. He followed her in and Tamzin introduced William as her fiancé, assuring him that he could speak freely in front of him. They sat down, then Chief Inspector Morris leaned forward, his voice tense.

'I'm afraid I have bad news for you all. As you know we had men waiting for Weston at his flat yesterday. I'm afraid he gave them the slip.'

'But how did he know they'd be there?' Tamzin asked.

'We'll never know the answer to that, Miss Thornham, but my guess is he just sensed something was wrong. Anyway, it leaves us with a very worrying situation. With his cunning he could evade us for quite some time and that leaves you in a vulnerable position,

Laura. He'll have realised by now that you helped us set a trap for him.'

'But could he come here?' Laura asked anxiously.

'It's possible he might try to make contact with you. In his twisted way Weston most likely thinks he could talk you out of testifying against him and I don't think he'd draw the line at some rather unpleasant intimidation.'

There was a stunned silence, then Tamzin said, 'But are you able to offer Laura some protection?'

'I can leave a couple of men here but I don't mind admitting that trying to protect someone who lives in a hotel is an operational nightmare. With people coming and going all the time it would be an almost impossible job.'

'What are you trying to tell me, Chief Inspector?' Laura asked.

'I have to lay it on the line for you, Laura. Whilst Weston is at large I don't think you are safe at Thornham House.'

8

It was Tamzin who broke the shocked silence, saying, 'Where do you expect Laura to go, Chief Inspector?'

'There is one simple remedy but I'm not sure what you'll think about it. Could you possibly go abroad, Laura? Is there anyone you could stay with?'

'I have friends in Paris,' Tamzin put in. 'What about Marie and Pierre, Laura. I'm sure they'd love to have you and you have all always got on well.'

'If you could fix it, sis, that would wonderful but . . . '

A frown settled on her brow as she addressed the Chief Inspector.

'How safe would I be in Paris? Surely Weston would simply have to jump on the shuttle.'

'Now, that's the beauty of my suggestion,' he replied. 'Even if Weston knew where you were he'd never reach you. Every port and airport will have his description and it's my guess that an old hand like Weston won't even try to skip the country. He'd know we'd have points of exits covered.

'Going abroad seems the best option, love,' William said to Laura but before they could discuss it further the doorbell rang.

'That'll be Mr Hunter,' Chief Inspector Morris said. 'He said he'd join us as soon as he could.'

Laura went to let him in and when he entered Chief Inspector Morris said, 'I've brought everyone up to date, Mr Hunter. I've also broached the subject of Laura going abroad.'

'And what does the lady in question think?' Rob asked.

'What the Chief Inspector says makes sense,' Laura said soberly, 'and Tamzin thinks Marie and Pierre would take me in.'

'That would be ideal,' Rob returned.

'I think I should go with you all the same,' Tamzin broke in. 'Marie and

Pierre are out a lot. I'd feel better if someone was there for you at all times.'

'Tamzin's got a point,' William said to Laura. 'Goodness knows how long this situation will continue. It would be more comfortable for you if you had someone from home with you.'

'I'll be perfectly all right,' Laura protested, a little too vehemently, Tamzin thought. 'Besides, Tamzin has her work at the hotel to consider. She can't just waltz off at a moment's notice.'

'I don't want to interfere in family matters,' the Chief Inspector said suddenly, 'but from a police point of view I would prefer it if Miss Thornham did not accompany her sister. I don't wish to appear sexist but I think it would be better if Laura was accompanied by a man. I'm reasonably certain we can prevent Weston from leaving the country but a wise copper always leaves room for doubt. To be on the safe side I would like Laura to be with a male friend who's fully conversant with the situation.'

The obvious choice was Rob and as Tamzin looked at him to gauge his reaction she was astonished to hear William speak up.

'In that case, I'll go with Laura and stay in Paris until the danger is over.'

'But what about your work?' Laura asked before Tamzin had a chance to speak. 'Your dad will go spare if you leave him in the lurch.'

'But I won't be. I can take my work with me. All I need is my laptop computer. I can work successfully in a Parisian apartment.'

'He's right, you know,' Tamzin said, backing William up. 'He's the ideal person to go with you and, I will be eternally grateful to him if he does.'

'That's settled then,' the Chief Inspector said, standing up. 'Please contact your friends and make your arrangements to leave as soon as possible. I'll feel a good deal more relaxed, Laura, when you're safely out of the country.'

He left, taking Rob with him, to leave the others to make phone calls and discuss their plans. Later, when William had departed to break the news to his father, Tamzin put her feet up.

'Look, sis,' Laura said as she sat opposite, 'I hope you don't mind William coming with me. It's only a matter of months before your wedding. Won't it disrupt all your plans?'

'Not really. I can continue to make arrangements and confer with William on the phone. We'll manage. All that matters is your safety, love. William was right to suggest it and he'll be good company for you.'

'Of course he will. We've always got on well. I wish I had your good taste in men. My poor judgement has brought terrible trouble to our family.'

'You were very young when you were targeted by Weston,' Tamzin pointed out. 'A lot of people would have fallen for his silvery tongue.'

Two days later, at the airport, when Tamzin was saying goodbye to William, she felt a pang of regret that she wasn't going with him. She would miss his companionship and although she couldn't entrust her sister to a better person she knew she would not rest easily until both were safely home again.

The hotel was in complete darkness when the police car dropped her back home in the early hours. She showered and fell into bed but, in spite of her exhaustion, found it impossible to sleep. The extraordinary events of the last few days reverberating through her mind.

She was just thinking of getting up and making tea when the sound of a door closing in the empty lumber room next door sent a shiver of fear through her. Moving as quietly as possible through the flat she stepped out into the corridor, pausing outside the door to the next room. Without stopping to think she twisted the knob, found it open, and then flung the door back. The room was brilliant lit and empty of all the dusty, broken furniture it had once been filled with. Instead, large cartons were stacked against the wall and Rob stood in front of her!

'Rob, you gave me the fright of my life! I thought we had an intruder and I must admit Daniel Weston swept through my mind,' she said angrily.

'Look, I'm really sorry I disturbed you. I was trying to be quiet.'

'I think you'd better tell me what's going on.'

He ushered her to a corner of the room where an electric fire threw out some heat and there was a small stool and a coffee table.

'It's quite simple, Tamzin. I'm having this room turned into a flatlet. I'll do all my work from the hotel and will stay here until Weston is captured.'

Tamzin digested his words in silence. She had assumed something of the sort as she had looked around the transformed room.

'So,' she said, 'you think I'm in need of protection.'

'I don't want to alarm you, Tamzin, but I know you are.'

'But why? What would Weston want with me?'

'Laura's whereabouts. You're the one person guaranteed to know.'

'Even so,' she said, 'moving into the hotel seems a drastic move on your part. I'm surrounded by people here.'

'But remember what the Chief Inspector said. Thornham House is open to all and sundry which leaves you pretty vulnerable, and there's no way the police will be able to grant twenty-four hour protection.'

'And you will?'

'I can give it a good try.'

'When did you empty this place?'

'Today, when you were at the airport. I didn't discuss it with you first, because I thought you might object.

'I appreciate your motives. Admittedly it goes against the grain to accept that I need protection, but we are faced with a rather formidable opponent in Weston. Rob, how long do you think he'll be free? If you're going to all this trouble to adapt this room you must think he'll be at large for a while.'

'I hope I'm wrong, Tamzin, but it is likely we'll have a long wait. I had quite a frank chat with the Chief Inspector. Weston has a formidable network of support in London. If he stays in the capital he can go underground for a considerable length of time.'

The prospect was utterly depressing. Exhaustion swept over her. She rose to her feet, stifling a yawn.

'I really must go and get some sleep now.'

Over the next few days, Henry organised extra staff to complete the adaptation of the lumber room into a basic, but serviceable, flat. Tamzin also received her first phone call from Laura and William and was pleased to hear they had received the best of welcomes from Marie and Pierre.

Tamzin replaced the receiver with a frown, wondering if she had been right not to mention Rob's presence at the hotel. She didn't like keeping things from Laura and William but she would have had to explain his motives and then her sister and her fiancé would realise that she was, potentially, in as much danger as themselves. It was better for them not to have the worry.

Tamzin found it strange to be without Laura, as well as William, over the succeeding weeks. Rob was now firmly settled in and when he wasn't busy with his own work he was often available for advice on the running of the hotel. They got into the habit of taking their morning coffee together and one morning Tamzin found herself bemoaning the lack of police success.

'Weston is still at large, Laura and William are still stuck in Paris, our lives have been turned upside down and the police seem to be doing nothing! I'm not convinced they are pulling out all the stops. Perhaps we should do something ourselves to flush Weston out.'

'I hope you're not suggesting we do

anything reckless?'

'Of course not,' Tamzin said briskly. 'I was just speculating, that's all.'

She realised, from Rob's reaction, that it would be pointless to continue the discussion, but over the next few days she considered what to do. Once again she knew she would have to act alone, without Rob's knowledge, but that would prove extremely difficult. She knew that, at some point, he would have to return to London to attend a board meeting and would need to stay overnight. That would give her forty-eight hours in which to act and she knew she could not afford to waste the opportunity. At last Rob served notice that he would be in London the following weekend. His next remark caught her off guard.

'So, perhaps you'd like to come with me. I know you're tired of being cooped up here.'

'Normally, I'd love to,' she said, attempting to inject regret into her voice, 'but you know how short-staffed we are at the moment.'

He seemed happy to accept her explanation. When she booked extra staff from an agency, she told Henry it was because she intended to go with Rob to London after all, but not to tell him as it was to be a surprise.

That evening, in the privacy of her apartment, she punched out a London number on her phone and spoke for several minutes. Concluding the conversation, she replaced the receiver with a smile. For good or ill, her plans were set. In a few days time, unknown to Rob, she would follow in his footsteps to the capital.

9

Tamzin seated herself opposite Harry Smith in the very same chair she'd used when she had first met the private detective months before.

'Does Mr Hunter know you're speaking to me?' he asked.

'Of course, we're working together on this. Has Rob updated you on what's been happening?' she asked.

'Yes. He's been in touch and so have the police. You were right about your father all along, Miss Thornham.'

'I was delighted he was exonerated, but at the expense of my sister.'

'From what I've heard, your sister didn't know what she was getting herself into. Besides, the police will be able to throw the book at Weston because of the help she's given.'

'If they ever catch him,' Tamzin sighed, 'and that's why I've come.'

She explained the situation they were in.

'I sympathise, Miss Thornham, but how can I help?'

'Last time I spoke to you I gained the impression you knew a good deal about Weston, probably more than the police. Now he's on the run I think you'd have a good idea whom he'd turn to. Could you give me names? The police have had weeks and weeks and they've drawn a blank. Please help me, Mr Smith. I'm desperate to get Laura home.'

He sighed, as though in capitulation, and said, 'One name, and one only, and make sure you do nothing until you've spoken with Mr Hunter.'

He wrote on the pad before him, ripped out the page, and handed it over.

'Thank you!'

Outside, she hailed a passing cab and then told the driver to go to the address on the notepaper. It was half an hour before the taxi stopped and the driver pointed out a high rise block of flats across the road. She climbed out, negotiated the busy road, then entered the lobby of the block of flats. It was unkempt and dimly lit, with no-one about, but when she entered the lift, to her relief, she found it working. At the tenth floor she stepped out to find another poorly-lit corridor, the numbers missing from most of the doors. The one she was looking for, however, was marked and as she pressed the door bell she hoped fervently for a response.

Within seconds she was aware she was being scrutinised through the spyhole in the door. The door opened a little and a man's face peered out at her, the expression guarded.

'Yes?'

'Larry Stevens?'

'Might be. Who's asking?' he replied.

'Tamzin Thornham. I'm here to ask you about Daniel Weston.'

'Never heard of him.'

'My informant tells me differently, Mr Stevens. Anyway, I'd like you to pass a message on to Mr Weston.'

'Can't do that if I've never heard of the guy, can I?'

She passed over a card with the details of where she was staying on it.

'Tell him it would be in his interests to talk to me. I'll be in all evening.'

Before he could respond she turned and left. Going down in the lift she wondered if her ploy had worked. Larry Stevens' protestations of ignorance had clearly been false and there had been a definite flicker of recognition when she had mentioned her name. She had little doubt that Larry Stevens was on the phone this very moment informing Daniel Weston of her visit.

She just hoped she had done enough to persuade Weston to make contact. And when he did, the police would be waiting for him. She stepped out of the lobby to face the roar of the London traffic. She needed somewhere quiet where she could use her mobile phone to contact Chief Inspector Morris and had no desire to step back into the gloomy lobby.

She was thinking of going straight back to her hotel when she spied an empty coffee shop. She hurried inside, collected a coffee at the counter, and then settled herself in the far corner before stabbing out the number she had learned by heart on her mobile. An unfamiliar voice answered.

'Sergeant Graves here.'

'Oh, I was expecting to speak to Chief Inspector Morris. This is Tamzin Thornham. He told me I could contact him on his mobile phone anytime.'

'Normally you can, madam, but the Chief Inspector is in court.'

'When will he be free?'

'Difficult to say, madam. It should be quite soon.'

'Then please give him a message to telephone me as soon as possible. It's most urgent.'

She told him the number of her mobile phone and then rang off. She drank her coffee and pondered her next move. It would be most unwise to return to her hotel until she had arranged police cover. Although she did not expect Weston to make a move until the evening she was still not prepared to sit, unprotected, in an empty hotel room. She would take a cab into central London, she decided, and while away the time sightseeing until she'd heard from the Chief Inspector.

It would be easier to hail a cab outside than to phone for one so she hurried out on to the pavement and began to watch the passing traffic. As luck would have it, a black cab was parked farther down the street. It rejoined the slow-moving traffic and as it drew to a halt beside her, Tamzin jumped in, issuing instructions to the driver as she did so. To her surprise, the cab did not move. Instead the driver turned around.

'Good afternoon, Miss Thornham.'

The baseball cap, pulled down low, obscured his features, but Tamzin had no doubt she was staring into the face of Daniel Weston! Her hand reached for the door but Weston's smile simply grew broader.

'I've locked them from the driver's seat.'

'Let me go,' she exclaimed.

'But why? I thought you wanted to speak to me.'

'I do,' Tamzin said, her heart pounding, 'but not under these circumstances. I thought we'd meet later at my hotel.'

'Oh, I'd no intention of meeting you on your terms but I was intrigued by what you said. You see, I was in the flat when you were at the door. I decided to follow you and when I saw you in that coffee shop I had the feeling you'd need a cab when you came out. So, I doubled back and picked up this vehicle. Larry earns an honest crust as a taxi driver!'

Weston took advantage of a gap in the traffic to shoot forward. Tamzin sat huddled in the corner, her thoughts in a whirl. She had no idea where Weston was taking her and no idea what his intentions were. Suddenly she remembered her mobile phone and slipped her hand inside her pocket. It wasn't there! She checked her other pocket and as she found it empty had a sudden image of it lying on the table in the café. She must have left it behind!

Weston turned sharply to the right. The housing now began to give way to bleak warehouses, many of them derelict and boarded up. Tamzin was unable to decipher the names of the streets they were speeding through. The car came to a sudden halt and Tamzin was almost thrown off her seat. The door opened and as she climbed out Weston's hand clamped on her upper arm.

'Time for that little chat, Miss Thornham.'

Weston was leading her towards a building with barred windows which looked completely derelict. He unlocked the door and when they stepped inside Tamzin had to make a conscious effort not to look surprised.

The long, low, room with white, newly-painted walls was comfortably furnished with contemporary, stylish furniture. She had no doubt she had just entered the refuge Weston used when he needed to lie low. No wonder he could disappear from sight for weeks on end. No-one would think this squalid, deserted looking building could house such an apartment.

Daniel Weston went around the room switching on lamps to relieve the gloom and then gestured for Tamzin to sit.

'OK, Miss Thornham, say what you have to say, and make it snappy.'

She knew it was crucial to persuade Weston that she was genuinely seeking terms.

'I'm here to speak for Laura,' she said.

'Oh, yeah? Why can't she speak for herself?'

'She can't. She's abroad. The police have been harassing her so much she's gone abroad to escape them.'

'I thought it was me they were after,

not your angelic-looking sister.'

'Look, Laura didn't want to help the police against you but they put her under terrible pressure. She regrets what she's done and she's willing to make amends, for a price.'

Understanding dawned on Weston's face.

'Now we're getting to it. How much does she want?'

'I'm sure we can come to some sort of arrangement,' she said desperately, adding, 'The case against you would collapse without my sister's testimony. You need her help and I can arrange that. Do you agree?'

'I agree that I need her help.'

'Good. I'll telephone Laura as soon as I get back to my hotel and tell her you're willing to play ball.'

'I don't think so. I think I can obtain your sister's co-operation without handing over my hard-earned cash. Of course, that would mean you would have to be my house guest for a while but I'd do my best to ensure your comfort. Laura will receive a simple offer — your safe return for a statement to my lawyer that she was forced by the police to entrap me. That will undermine anything they try to throw at me. Good thinking, eh?'

'You could make things much worse for yourself if you attempt to keep me here against my will.'

'Don't be so melodramatic. I'm simply offering you my hospitality for a few days. And if you should take it into your head to lay a charge against me you'll find that I have a cast-iron alibi for the time in question.'

Tamzin digested his words in silence, then decided, for the moment, it would be unwise to provoke him further.

'Now, if you can give me Laura's telephone number I'll contact her and get things moving,' he said.

'I don't have the number,' she said, playing for time. 'It's in my address book back at the hotel.'

'Really? I suspect you know it off by heart.'

He glanced down at his watch then stood up.

'I have to be somewhere. When I get back I hope to find that your memory has improved.'

Next moment he was gone, the sound of the lock turning in the door a depressing reminder of the hopelessness of her position. She crossed to the barred window in time to see a white car drive past. Weston must have switched to another vehicle for she could still see the taxi parked outside.

Tamzin knew she had no time to waste if she was to effect an escape. She made a quick check of the other rooms. As expected, there was no phone anywhere and the flat consisted of a small, windowless bedroom, a tiny bathroom and a small kitchenette which looked out on to a back yard full of rubbish and surrounded by a brick wall, broken glass set into the top.

The kitchen window was wide and rectangular, but again barred, whilst a scrutiny of the door revealed that it had a yale lock only. It might just be possible to force it open. Tamzin pulled open drawer after drawer until she came across the cutlery. She chose the strongest looking knife and then set to work.

Half an hour later she flung her utensil down in disgust and looked in despair at the door which refused to budge in spite of all her efforts. In that bleak, despairing moment she longed for only one person, Rob. She yearned for the comfort of his presence and the feel of his strong arms around her. She didn't question her need, she just knew in that revealing moment that she loved him, and that she had always loved him.

But it was no time to start dwelling on her tangled emotional life. She must thrust aside all personal thoughts and concentrate her mind on getting out of here! She leaned back and as she looked upwards it struck her, as though for the first time, that a modern, suspended ceiling ran throughout the single storey flat. They had used such ceilings when converting Thornham House into a hotel and she knew the large, rectangular tiles were light and easily lifted.

She leaped to her feet, her mind already working on how she could reach up to the ceiling safely. She went into the kitchen, placed a chair on to the draining board and then stood back. As long as she was careful it should give her a secure foothold for entry into the roof area, she decided.

Tamzin needed to do one more thing before she could get started. She must find some light. She thought of the most logical place to keep a torch. Most people kept torches in case of a power cut so if Weston had one it would most likely be near the fuse box!

She found the fuse box in a slim cupboard, and when she opened the door, a torch rolled out. Eagerly she switched it on, and though the beam was weak, it was a good deal better than nothing. Now she was ready and she used a stool to climb on to the sink unit. Clasping the back of the chair to steady herself she stepped gingerly on to the seat.

She was now crouching beneath the ceiling and as she straightened, she pushed at the ceiling tile with the palm of her hands. Just as she had hoped, it lifted easily and she pushed it to one side. The upper part of her body was now inside the roof space. She pulled the torch out of her pocket and as the thin beam lit up the area in front of her, she realised, with growing excitement, that her hunch might just have paid off.

Weston's apartment and the building next door must at one time have been one building for there was no wall to partition the roof area. What's more, she could detect a faint trace of light about twenty feet in front of her. It looked as though there might be an opening in the rear wall of the neighbouring building. All she needed to do was investigate, and quickly.

The ceiling tiles would never take her weight but there were enormous beams running in the direction she needed to go. Resting her weight on her hands she pulled her legs up behind her, kneeling briefly on a ceiling tile, before clambering on to the beam adjacent to the rear wall. She began the slow journey, the torch clasped precariously in one hand. It seemed like hours but must have been only a matter of minutes before she reached the square of light which seemed to get bigger as she approached.

She rested on her haunches and contemplated the rectangle of light made by several missing bricks. She had been hoping for some sort of window that she could climb through but as she took in the state of the bricks, she realised she might be able to dislodge others to make a much larger space. In a matter of minutes, Tamzin had created an opening wide enough to crawl through. But how far off the ground was she?

Gingerly she peered through the gap to find herself looking down at a concrete yard. A fall from such a height could break bones but there was a heap of rubbish consisting of piles of newspapers and cardboard boxes piled up against the wall to the right. Before her nerve failed her she crouched at the opening, facing the way she intended to fall. She pushed herself forward, head first, and the next moment the breath was knocked out of her body as she landed on the garbage. She was up in a flash, fear of Weston's return far greater than any concern for bumps and bruises. Now she had got into this yard, could she get out of it?

As Tamzin cleared a path through the rubbish she could see a door, partially open and sagging on its hinges in front of her. A few more steps and she'd be free! Next moment, her mood of euphoria was burst as she heard the distinct sound of a man's footsteps coming towards her. Weston must have returned, realised what she had done and come after her to head her off! She looked round for a weapon and her eyes fell on an old wooden table leg. She picked it up then stood next to the door, her back flat against the wall and her right hand, with the weapon in it, raised high above her head.

The footsteps came to a halt. Next moment Tamzin's heart beat a tattoo as the door swung slowly open. As Tamzin prepared to rain blows down on the tall figure now stepping into the yard, the man turned suddenly, his arm raised to shield himself from the blow and a familiar, and beloved voice rang out, 'It's me, Tamzin. Rob!'

The weapon fell from her hand and she gazed on him, eyes wide with wonderment. A sob rose within her at the thought of how close she had come to causing him serious harm and next moment he was pulling her into his arms and she was giving vent to her emotions as hot tears scalded her cheeks. He attempted to soothe her with gentle words.

10

It was bliss to be in Rob's arms and in those few moments all the fear and hurt of the traumatic day seemed to seep away. Yet they were both still in danger and Tamzin looked up at Rob, her eyes apprehensive.

'Rob, Weston could come back at any moment. We need to get away!'

He caught her hand and led her through the alleyway which ran along the back of the properties out on to the main road. His car was parked at the kerbside and he settled her into the passenger seat.

As they roared off he said, 'I want to get you as far away from this godforsaken place as fast as the speed limit will allow.'

'There's one thing we must do, though,' Tamzin said, 'and that is to inform the police about Weston's whereabouts. He's due back at his flat any time now. If they lie in wait for him they can catch him.'

'Do you know Chief Inspector Morris's number?'

'Yes, I know it by heart.'

'Good, then telephone him on the car phone and explain the situation. Then hand the phone to me and I'll give him directions to Weston's flat.

Tamzin felt immense relief when the Chief Inspector himself answered. He listened without interrupting and then she passed the phone over to Rob. When he'd finished, he looked over at Tamzin with a smile.

'Now, are you going to tell me how you found me, Rob?'

'Just wait until we get to my flat. It's not far from here and I think you'll feel all the better for a meal and a shower. Then we'll exchange stories.'

Rob was right, she decided later, as she tucked her feet beneath her and settled back comfortably into an armchair. As if on cue, the kitchen door swung back and Rob entered carrying the coffee tray which he unloaded on to the low table.

'I'm holding you to your word, Rob. It's time you explained everything. How on earth did you track me down?'

Rob seated himself opposite her.

'Harry Smith must have got cold feet after your visit and he called me to confirm that I did know of your investigations. No way did I know! I tried you on your mobile straight away and got some bewildered café owner who'd seen you leave in a taxi but had no idea where you'd gone. When I asked for the address of the café the alarm bells started to ring! I knew it was close to Larry Stevens' address and could only conclude that you'd followed the lead Harry had given you and gone to see him.'

'I was wrong to act alone,' Tamzin said, shamefacedly.

'You were crazy! Anyway, I went straight round to Larry Stevens' place. I think he sensed my determination and

170

when he found out you'd been seen leaving a local coffee shop in a taxi I could see that he was really worried. I pointed out that if he was in anyway involved he could be liable for aiding and abetting an abduction but emphasised that I could put in a good word for him with the police if he helped me. Finally, I employed a tactic which, thankfully, the police can't use.'

'Which is?'

'Cash. In his twisted way I think taking money off me made him think he was co-operating on his own terms. He told me everything. I was then convinced that Weston had picked you up in Larry's taxi in the hope of getting to Laura through you.'

'I'm afraid I walked straight into Weston's trap. I'd intended to set myself up as bait to lure Weston to my hotel where the police would be waiting. I hadn't bargained on Weston already being at Larry's place.'

'I don't think Weston would ever have walked into such a trap.'

'To my cost, I realise that now. Anyway,' she said, 'why didn't you contact the police as soon as you had Weston's address?'

'I had a great fear that police tactics might put you in danger so I decided to spy out the land first. I had no number for Weston's place, just the name of the street but when I arrived and saw the taxi I guessed which flat must be his. I couldn't see anything through that barred window so decided to check out the rear. I was walking down the back alley, trying to find my bearings, when I heard the sound of smashing bricks. It was that racket which led me to you, Tamzin. And now it's your turn to tell your story.'

Tamzin relayed everything that had happened and when she had finished he shook his head in disbelief.

'You know, Tamzin, I should be furious with you for risking your life but I have to admit I admire your guts and spirit. I'm just glad you're on my side!'

'I wonder when we'll hear from the police.'

'Not until tomorrow, I hope. You need a good night's sleep and the spare bedroom awaits you.'

Tamzin complied thankfully. She was exhausted and slept late the following morning. When she emerged it was to find Chief Inspector Morris there, deep in conversation with Rob. He rose at her approach.

'Good news, my dear. Following your tip off we picked Weston up late last night. He's safely in police custody. You and your family are quite safe. I can't condone taking the law into your own hands, Miss Thornham, but I am grateful to you for handing Weston to us on a plate.'

The Chief Inspector explained that they were both required to make statements and must remain in London for the next few days. These days were hectic as they helped the police as much as possible. Over this time Tamzin made several phone calls to

Paris and was puzzled when there was no reply. She expressed her puzzlement to Rob when they travelled back down to Devon together on the train. He dismissed her worries.

'I daresay they've gone away for a few days. People do, you know.'

'I've left a message on Marie's answerphone.'

Marie returned Tamzin's call a few days later. She and Pierre had been visiting relatives and when Tamzin explained the purpose of her phone call whoops of joy filled the line.

'I can't wait to tell Laura and William,' Tamzin went on. 'Can you put one of them on?'

'Chèrie, did you not know? They are in the South of France for a week or two. They needed a break, so I suggested they go in search of some sun.'

Tamzin wondered, momentarily, why they hadn't mentioned it.

'Have you a contact number?' she asked.

'I'm afraid not. They're moving around, but I'm sure they'll be in touch soon. If they telephone here I'll tell them the good news.'

As she replaced the receiver Tamzin was struck with the irony that whilst she and Rob had risked life and limb to bring about a speedy end to their difficulties, Laura and William were now swanning around the South of France. Rob, once more, put her concerns into perspective.

'They've been under a great strain, Tamzin. I daresay they went off on the spur of the moment in order to cheer themselves up.'

He was right of course, and she was churlish to quibble, but another week went by without news from Laura and William. Tamzin longed for, yet dreaded, their return. It would be wonderful to see them but it would mean a resumption of her wedding plans and since her realisation that it was Rob she loved, the thought of marriage to William filled her with apprehension.

Would it be fair to William to marry him knowing she loved another man? But would it be fair to break his heart? She concluded that she was duty bound to honour her promise to William and also to ensure that he was never aware that her feelings for him were anything less than heartfelt.

At last Tamzin received the long-awaited phone call from Paris. Surprisingly it was Marie who called to say that William and Laura had been thrilled to hear of Weston's capture and were making hasty plans to return. When Tamzin asked to speak to one of them she was told they were packing and as they intended to hire a car at the airport, not to worry about picking them up. It was strange not to hear this news from them personally but now she knew they'd be home in a few days. She set off to find Rob.

He was on the West Terrace, leaning against the balustrade and gazing across the parkland. He turned at her approach.

'You've heard from Paris?'

'Yes. William and Laura will be back with us in a few days.'

'Soon you'll be re-united with William and be able to resume your wedding plans.'

She wished she could have sounded a little more enthusiastic as she said, 'Yes, and it will be wonderful to see them both again.'

'I, too, have been thinking of my future. I'm no longer needed at Thornham House.'

'Well, I suppose you'll be moving back to London now.'

'A little farther afield than that. I intend to return to Canada. It is my homeland after all.'

The shock must have registered on her face for he said, 'Don't look so alarmed, Tamzin. I'm not going to leave you and Henry in the lurch. My deputy will take over the European side of things.'

For once in her life Tamzin had not been thinking of the fortunes of Thornham House. She was thinking of the effects on her heart! She tried to mask her inner turmoil as she spoke.

'I know your company will always deal fairly with us, Rob. I was surprised that you were giving up your life in Britain. You've always seemed so at home here.'

'Things change, and now I want a new direction to my life.'

'When will you go?' she asked in a small voice.

'I'll return to London tomorrow, sort a few things out, then I expect to be flying to Canada within a week.'

Tamzin made an excuse about having to see Henry but hurried straight back to her apartment. As the door closed behind her she broke down, tears streaming down her face. It was for the best, she told herself repeatedly. She could never be Rob's so did it matter whether he was in London or across the Atlantic? But the thought of him being so far away broke her heart.

As Rob left Thornham House the next day, he pecked her on the cheek.

'Be happy,' he said.

She could barely reply but the next moment he was in his car and driving away, Tamzin's pale face and strained expression going unnoticed.

She kept herself extremely busy over the next few days. Returning late one evening after a business appointment she opened the door to the flat to find the light on in the passageway. That could mean only one thing! Sure enough, the sitting-room door opened and next moment Laura was flinging herself into her arms. Tamzin was surprised to see tears in her sister's eyes.

'Tell me everything,' Laura urged. 'I gather you were instrumental in capturing Weston.'

They settled themselves comfortably in the sitting-room and Tamzin relayed all that had happened to her.

'You did all that for me and William?'

Laura said, as Tamzin's tale came to an end. 'Oh, Tamzin! I don't deserve you as a sister, I really don't.'

'Hey,' Tamzin said, 'the bad times are over now. Let's all look forward to a brighter future.'

For some reason this set Laura off again and it was several minutes before she could compose herself. Tamzin tried to change her mood by asking about Paris but Laura said she had been travelling all day and felt too tired to talk about it.

Tamzin then went into the kitchen to make tea, and as she did, it struck her that neither of them had mentioned William. As he was her fiancé it was she who should really have asked about him but it was strange that Laura had remained silent as well. Presumably he had gone to his parents and would come over tomorrow.

So it proved. Soon after Laura departed for the swimming pool, William arrived. Tamzin was shocked to see how thin he looked. He kissed her on the cheek, settled himself on the couch, and once more Tamzin relayed her story. William, too, seemed unwilling to be drawn further on their time in France and Tamzin could only conclude, sadly, that this reticence must, in part, be due to the stresses and strains they had both endured.

Over the next two weeks Laura made it clear she was anxious to get her career back on track and threw herself into her duties, so much so, that Tamzin began to worry for her health as she worked long hours, with few breaks. William, too, had a good deal of work to catch up on at his father's firm and when he and Tamzin did see each other it was for snatched moments in which they decided the final details for the wedding which was now only two months away.

William seemed happy to leave most of the decisions to her but when they went to see the vicar, he seemed ill at ease. Tamzin knew she must make allowances for the fact that William was still adjusting to normal life after his time away.

A few days later, Tamzin decided to take some time off and do some coastal walking. She chose a cove in the next village along, not an area she usually frequented. The beach of hard sand was an ideal one for walking along and she negotiated a steep path down on to the shoreline and then set off at a brisk pace.

She was keeping close to the edge of the cliffs and as she turned a bend she was confronted by the sight of two figures. They were oblivious to her presence and as she made to call out to them the words died in her throat. It was William and Laura! The wind whipped their words away but from their demeanour it was obvious they were having a furious quarrel.

It seemed such a private moment that Tamzin felt she ought to tip-toe away. The next moment William had pulled Laura into his arms as though he never wanted to let her go and she was clinging on to him as though she was a part of him. In that heart-stopping moment Tamzin realised what had happened, and she also knew what she had to do.

She walked closer and they sensed her presence at last, pulling apart, horror written across their faces. Laura opened her mouth to speak but Tamzin halted her by laying one finger against her lips.

She took Laura's hand and then William's. First she looked at William.

'I think the time is right, William, to tell you I have never loved you as much as you deserve to be loved. It was unfair of me to agree to be your wife. I can guess that you have found true love now with my sister, and I wish you both joy.'

She joined both their hands together and next moment all three of them were hugging, laughing and crying all at the same time.

★   ★   ★

'I've no idea how it happened,' Laura confided to Tamzin later as they talked well into the night. 'You know I've always been terribly fond of William but I regarded him as your property. I was too busy getting involved with unsuitable men to appreciate what was there in front of me all along.'

'You wouldn't have been ready for William at an earlier age,' Tamzin said shrewdly. 'You had a lot of growing up to do and your experiences over the last months, although painful, have changed you quite a lot.'

'That's true,' Laura admitted. 'Anyway, when we were in Paris, William gave me the most tremendous emotional support. I grew to depend on him, and before I had a chance to reign in my emotions I realised my feelings for him had grown. But I had no intention of stealing my sister's fiancé! I deliberately withdrew from him and when William became upset I knew, instinctively, that he had fallen in love with me, too. We confessed our love, but we also decided that nothing could come of it.'

Laura dabbed at her eyes with her handkerchief, drew a deep breath, then continued.

'Like you, William had realised by then that his feelings for you were based on affectionate friendship but it would have mortified him to hurt you. The holiday we took in Provence was to be our swan song, our last chance to be together before we reverted to our rôles as old friends.'

'And then you were recalled to England.'

'Yes. We decided it would be easier on ourselves if we avoided each other as much as possible. When you met us on the beach yesterday we'd just snatched a few moments together. I was telling William that I intended to go abroad straight after your wedding and we were just having a furious row about it when you showed up.'

'And thank goodness I did. The prospect of William and me marrying out of a sense of duty when neither of us truly loved each other doesn't bear thinking about.'

'Just why did you agree to marry William in the first place, Tamzin? From what you've said you've always had doubts.'

Tamzin looked down, the colour of her cheeks betraying her discomfort. She had not confided her feelings about Rob to Laura. She didn't want Laura worrying about her disastrous love life when she had so much to look forward to herself.

'I was at a rather low ebb at the time,' she said. 'William was being incredibly supportive and it just seemed right to agree to his proposal. Once I'd said yes I felt committed, but you know, I've always loved William more as a brother and now that's exactly what he'll become!'

The two sisters beamed at one another.

They had an awkward few days in which they had to explain to relatives and friends the unconventional change of plan but once people had got over the shock and realised that Tamzin was entirely happy with the arrangement people soon accepted the situation. Tamzin went with William and Laura to see the vicar and once he, too, had come round to the news he very generously agreed to allow William to retain the June booking at the church, albeit with a different bride! Tamzin now found herself stepping into the rôle of being chief bridesmaid.

The wedding dawned a golden June day and the sun beamed down as Laura and William walked out of the doors of their ancient, local church as man and wife to greet well wishers and pose for photographs. Tamzin had never seen Laura, or William, look so happy. Her eyes misted with joy, wishing that her father could have been there to share this moment with them.

She left the happy throng, and wandered over to the quiet corner of the churchyard where her father's grave lay. She crouched, laying her bouquet on his grave and saying a short prayer as she did so.

'Victor would have been very proud of his beautiful daughters today.'

She straightened slowly. Were her ears playing tricks?

'Aren't you going to look at me, Tamzin?'

She turned. She wasn't dreaming. Rob, in a beige suit, with a red carnation in his button hole, was standing before her. As though he sensed her disbelief he tapped his arm with one hand.

'I'm flesh and blood, Tamzin, not an apparition.'

'I . . . I didn't really expect to see you today,' she stammered.

'No? I was sent an invitation, although I admit I didn't open it when it first arrived. You see, I assumed it was for your wedding to William and that was something I just didn't want to think about.'

'So, when did you open it?'

'Only two days ago. I'd thrown it in my desk drawer and when my secretary was doing some tidying up, she opened it and left it out for me. I found it first thing when I got into work that morning and one name jumped right out at me — Laura Thornham. She was to be the lucky bride, not you! I got straight on to Henry and he filled me in on all the details. I flew to New York and took Concorde over. I wanted to be here to wish William and Laura joy and to see if some of their luck would rub off on me.'

'Oh, Rob,' Tamzin said tremulously, 'I've missed you so much!'

The next moment, she was in his arms and he was kissing her as though he would never let her go. At last they drew apart, Rob's voice shaky as he spoke.

'I guess that pretty well shows my feelings for you, my darling, but what about you? Can I dare to hope you feel the same?'

'Oh, Rob, I love you with all my heart!'

The smile in Rob's eyes seemed to reach into his very soul.

'Well, whilst everyone's in a wedding mood shall we try to catch that vicar of yours and see if he can find a space in the calendar for another happy couple?'

Tamzin's face revealed her joy as they began to walk, hand in hand, towards the sunlit church.

THE END

CONVALESCENT HEART

Lynne Collins

They called Romily the Snow Queen, but once she had been all fire and passion, kindled into loving by a man's kiss and sure it would last a lifetime. She still believed it would, for her. It had lasted only a few months for the man who had stormed into her heart. After Greg, how could she trust any man again? So was it likely that surgeon Jake Conway could pierce the icy armour that the lovely ward sister had wrapped about her emotions?

TOO MANY LOVES

Juliet Gray

Justin Caldwell, a famous personality of stage and screen, was blessed with good looks and charm that few women could resist. Stacy was a newcomer to England and she was not impressed by the handsome stranger; she thought him arrogant, ill-mannered and detestable. By the time that Justin desired to begin again on a new footing it was much too late to redeem himself in her eyes, for there had been too many loves in his life.

MYSTERY AT MELBECK

Gillian Kaye

Meg Bowering goes to Melbeck House in the Yorkshire Dales to nurse the rich, elderly Mrs Peacock. She likes her patient and is immediately attracted to Mrs Peacock's nephew and heir, Geoffrey, who farms nearby. But Geoffrey is a gambling man and Meg could never have foreseen the dreadful chain of events which follow. Throughout her ordeal, she is helped by the local vicar, Andrew Sheratt, and she soon discovers where her heart really lies.